MOON BONES

A NELLIE BURNS AND MOONSHINE MYSTERY

Novels by Julie Weston

NELLIE BURNS AND MOONSHINE MYSTERY SERIES:

Moonshadows

Basque Moon

Moonscape

Miners' Moon

Moon Bones

MOON BONES

A NELLIE BURNS AND MOONSHINE MYSTERY

JULIE WESTON

Julie Weston

Encircle Publications,
Farmington, Maine, U.S.A.

Paperback ISBN-13: 978-1-64599-412-1
Hardcover ISBN-13: 978-1-64599-410-7
E-book ISBN-13: 978-1-64599-411-4

Library of Congress Control Number: 2022943367

Cover design by Deirdre Wait
Cover photographs © Gerry Morrison

Published by:

Encircle Publications
PO Box 187
Farmington, ME 04938

info@encirclepub.com
http://encirclepub.com

For Gerry

Prologue

THE TRAIL WOUND ALONG A rocky empty streambed to the "x" marked on the map for gold and through lodgepole pines and aspen trees, bitterbrush and occasional sagebrush. Sammy Ah Kee followed his friend who carried the crumpled map in his back pocket. As Sammy ducked low to miss the backlash of springing branches, he wished he were back in the sagebrush hills of the Wood River Valley, where he could see for miles around. Claustrophobia in the thick trees and heavy underbrush slowed his steps and inspired beads of sweat on his forehead. He began to fall behind.

Over and down a ridge, Sammy heard the rush of water. The Salmon River flowed north through the Stanley Basin, but this would be a tributary flushed with spring snow melt. Hung Lui, also from Hailey, the mining town along the Big Wood River, once teeming with miners but now mostly sheep and sheep herders, said the flowing river would be easy to pan for gold. The pack on Sammy's back weighed too much, he thought. So did his misgivings about traipsing after Hung Lui. His mother was probably right. He stopped. He could go back and sell his gold panning equipment to some other fool.

"Sam. Come, come." Hung Lui's voice bounced off the thick tree trunks. "We almost there."

This man did not have a mother or Nellie Burns the photographer to teach him English as Sammy did. He and Hung Lui had crossed the Canadian border together and both settled in central Idaho. Ah Kee, Sammy's father, made sure they found work and obeyed all the laws and kept out of trouble. Now, without Ah Kee to keep discipline, the local Chinese in Hailey fell out of favor with the townspeople and many left town. Hung Lui laundered clothes and linens, not well but better than the white men. Sammy repaired shoes, learning the trade from the cobbler who hired him.

Sammy shrugged and resettled his pack. "I am coming," he called. "Wait for me."

When they reached the water, Hung Lui said, "Not here. Up path to creek. Gold waits there." He grinned at Sammy and shifted his own pack. "Not far." He added several words in Chinese, but Sammy had lost most of his native language, and it was a different dialect than his anyway.

"Speak American," he reminded Hung. "Learn better." He sometimes slipped into short words when his mother wasn't around to correct him.

"Up a creek," Hung said, hurrying along the rocky shore. "Man with gold in Hailey say."

The man had been another Chinese, so Hung trusted him. Sammy wasn't so sure. They had split the cost of the map.

The two men bushwhacked through green salal and thorn-laden bitterbrush and arrived at a creek, tumbling with snowmelt. To their surprise, four Chinese lined the creekside, all kneeling, all with pans they dipped and swished.

"Huh. Secret!" Hung spit.

Sammy watched the men. One he recognized from Ketchum or Hailey. The rest were strangers to him.

"We go higher," Hung Lui said. He swept his arm past the men toward where the creek tumbled in white streams down over rock. With a nod, Sammy edged along the creek in front of his friend and past the men, only one of whom seemed to spare them a look. Sammy's coat caught on sticker branches and his boots tangled in brush. His hat fell several times. He pulled it off, but then the tentacles of trees and bushes grabbed at his hair. When he replaced the flat, round hat, it stayed for the pace of twelve steps. It fell again. When he bent over to retrieve it, he fell. He was so disgusted, he stayed down, rolling over to sit on his haunches and wait for Hung. This was a wild crane chase. One day and then he would leave.

Wasps and bees hummed. The water splashed and tumbled, an irregular but soothing sound. A few birds sang chirpy songs back and forth. Sunlight warmed his back and his eyes closed. When he opened his eyes again, Sammy noticed the sun had moved and he was now in shade. He must have slept. Where was Hung Lui? Slowpoke.

He called Hung's name. The insects continued to buzz, the water to chatter. No birds until he finally heard a raven's raucous cry—just one. He sighed and crawled to his feet. Maybe Hung Lui had fallen, just as Sammy had done. Or maybe he stopped to pan for gold and assumed Sammy would do the same. Sammy walked back through the underbrush to see where his friend was. A fine friend, letting Sammy just wander off into the wilds.

After a while, Sammy recognized the stretch of creek where the four men had worked. They were gone. Hung Lui was gone, too, or at least Sammy hadn't seen him on his backtrack. Now what to do. It was late to start back to the trailhead, if he could ever find it. Why would Hung Lui leave him? As Sammy made his way down the creek, he noticed a large dark rock in the water. Strange. The water burbled and filled and emptied, so it inflated like a balloon—puff, collapse, puff, collapse. He splashed out to see what it was. What it was stopped him. A coolie coat filled and spilled. It covered a man's back and his head bobbed back and forth with the current. Sammy grabbed at the blue cloth and pulled the body to the creek's edge. He saw that the man's throat had been slashed so his neck opened like a fish's mouth. Then Sammy realized it was Hung Lui.

Chapter 1

NELLIE BURNS FLIPPED THROUGH A stack of negatives, trying to decide which to print first. She planned a trip to Twin Falls and Jacob Levine's photography studio later in the week and she wanted to be as efficient as possible. His generosity in loaning his darkroom to her seemed to know no bounds. A twinge of guilt slowed her organizing the photos from North Idaho. She must tell him she is engaged. Would that knowledge make him less generous?

A whisper of sound penetrated her planning. Nellie lifted her head to listen. Her landlady Goldie had gone to buy groceries. The other boarders traveled to the Triumph Mine for work. Only Henry, the retired miner, was still upstairs from her studio on the first floor. The noise sounded closer—the front door. Maybe Goldie needed help with packages. Nellie left the salon which held her studio, thanks to Goldie's generosity—so many people who were kind to her, a transplant from Chicago over a year ago.

When she swung the door open, expecting Goldie, Nellie's eyes opened wide. She lowered them to the small, once-strong image of Mrs. Ah Kee, the widow of the herbalist Ah Kee, whom Nellie had photographed *memento mori* for her. Sammy's mother and her own benefactor when Nellie lay so ill with pneumonia.

"Mrs. Ah Kee! What's wrong?" Only something dire would

have brought the Chinese woman to Ketchum to Nellie's door.

"Sammy, my son. He is gone!" Mrs. Ah Kee grasped Nellie's hand like a tentacle of talons. Her fingernails were grimy. "Is he here?" She stepped into the hallway, almost colliding with Nellie and made to dash up the stairs.

Nellie grabbed her jacket, a dark brocade, not material purchased in Hailey or Ketchum. "No, he is not here!"

"He has disappeared. I waited and waited, but he is gone." Tears began to flow down the crevasses of Mrs. Ah Kee's face. She began shaking and almost fell over at Nellie's feet.

"Mrs. Ah Kee. Come and rest. Tell me what has happened." Nellie released her grip on the old woman's jacket, placed her arm around shoulders that felt spiked with bones and led the widow to her studio. "I'll get you tea. We'll sort this out. Please wait just a few minutes."

The elderly Chinese woman nodded and brushed her tears away. Nellie dashed to the kitchen to heat water on the ever-warm kitchen woodstove. She returned as fast as possible with a teapot, cups and tea caddy. Her visitor sat slumped forward and at first Nellie thought she had fainted, or worse.

"Mrs. Ah Kee." Nellie gently nudged her. "I'm back. This tea will help." Nellie poured a cup and thought she might have to hold it to her visitor's lips, but Mrs. Ah Kee straightened and reached for the cup. She took tentative sips and her head nodded in a motion hardly discernible.

"Ah, you make good tea." Her voice rasped.

"I watched you make it for me." Nellie poured herself a cup. "Now, tell me about Sammy, please."

"You are… a… how do you say… assistant to that sheriff. You can find Sammy. Please find him. He is all I have left. He must send his father's bones to China." Once again, she clutched at Nellie.

"I will help if I can." Nellie shuddered at the mention of Ah Kee's bones. She remembered all too well how she had felt his bone under the snow where he had been buried. And later, when she took a photograph of him at Mrs. Ah Kee's demand, how his bald head resembled a moon with the deep cleft in it. "Where do you think Sammy is?"

"He wanted to find gold." Mrs. Ah Kee almost spat the word out, as if "gold" were poisonous. "He believed a pirate's story of gold over the Galena pass. Galena is lead, not gold!" Her voice raised and she placed her hand on her forehead and moaned. "How could my Sammy leave me?"

Stories of mines and gold, lead, and silver filled the Wood River Valley and the Stanley Basin north of Ketchum. But only one mine still operated—the Triumph mine, right there in the Wood River valley between Ketchum, where Nellie was, and south to Hailey, where the Ah Kees lived. Only lead and silver disgorged out of there. As far as Nellie knew, the gold prospecting in both places ended years before. "Did he tell you where he expected to find gold?" Nellie, too, thought Sammy had been tricked by tall tales. "Who took him there?"

"Hung Lui, the laundry worker. He told Sammy false stories—about panning for gold, riches to make them wealthy. Lies, all of it. I tried to talk Sammy out of following dreams of riches. He would not listen."

The little woman began to sob and dropped her cup. "Who will dig up the bones and send them to Guangdong? That honor must be performed or my husband's ghost will wander forever in this wicked place."

Nellie dropped to her knees to rescue the cup, fortunately empty of tea. "It sounds as if he went to the Stanley Basin. I will borrow an automobile, and we can motor up that way to see if anyone has seen Sammy." Few liked the Chinese in Idaho, except those, like herself, who had spent time with them. In the past, numbers of Chinese had been massacred, mostly in the abandoned mining areas, west and north of Ketchum and Hailey. A shiver raised the hair on Nellie's neck. Surely, people were more civilized now.

"No, no. I cannot go with you. People hate the Chinese. They want us dead. Ah Kee and I spirited Sammy here, through Canada, because he was not allowed to enter any of the ports on the ocean. Do you know how dreadful the whites are to us?"

Nellie knew of the Chinese Exclusion Acts but had not given them much thought. The Chinese in cities lived in Chinatowns and kept to themselves. But she saw how terribly the Negroes were often treated and the horrendous riots a few years ago in Chicago had killed many of the colored people. Irishmen built the railroad from the East and Chinese built it from the West. She had been surprised at the vehemence of townspeople in Idaho toward them. Otherwise, ever since her first exposure to the Ah Kees and taking photos at their behest, she had been removed from them, except for occasional English lessons with Sammy. Rather, she followed crimes with Sheriff Azgo—Charlie—now her fiancé. A feeling of warmth spread through her.

"I know. All right, I'll go alone and see what I can find out. I have met several people in the area." Pearl, the saloon girl, and Ned, the cowboy, were both gone. Pearl's erstwhile husband or lover was in jail. Cable O'Donnell—he, too, was gone. Maybe she didn't know anyone anymore.

* * *

Nellie borrowed the old automobile belonging to Henry. She turned down the retired miner's offer to drive her, accompanied by a half leer that disappeared when she said no. She didn't know how long she'd be gone, but she had some people to see at Galena Pass and then in Stanley. She might have asked to borrow Rosy's auto, but he wasn't in town at the moment. He also was a retired miner she had met when she first arrived in Ketchum. Now he worked as a deputy to the sheriff, at least for the time being. He would have insisted on going with her. She knew Rosy's auto could make it up and over Galena, but she wasn't sure Henry's would, even if she backed up the steep road at the Pass.

At the Galena store, Nellie stopped to say hello to Lulu, who was busy with greenhorns wanting cowboy boots and hats. Easterners, she thought, glad she was now a westerner. She poked around the store and looked at the locked display case with revolvers in it. That was something new in the store since her last visit about a year ago. They were not on open display then. It was time she owned one of her own.

When the customers were fully outfitted, one with a gunbelt he wore too high, Lulu sidled over. Nellie admired her western look, from her short haircut to her leather vest and skirt. She wore boots, but not cowboy boots. Her manner was friendly, but also no-nonsense with the tourists.

"Hello, Miss Burns. Haven't seen you in quite a while." She looked down at the hardware. "You can buy one this time if you like. Here, I'll open up and you can inspect the wares."

"I'm not sure what I want, but yes, it is time I owned some protection. I've been helping the sheriff, a sort of assistant deputy, but the town won't pay for—" she said and gestured to the display. "Can you advise me?"

"Where is your nice black dog?"

"Left him at home. I didn't think I'd need him for this project." Nellie didn't want to say that Moonshine disliked strange men.

Back by the now-opened gun case, Nellie listened while Lulu explained the finer points of the different models of revolvers. "If I was you, I'd get the lighter one with a quick action. Easy to load and unload. We can go out back and fire it a few times."

"I'm looking for a lost person, a friend, probably over in the Basin, so I can't take the time now, Lulu. Maybe on my way back." She picked up her camera pack from the floor beside her. "Have you seen any Chinese around here lately? I'm looking for Sammy Ah Kee."

"Don't know him. There were several Chinamen here a few days ago." She leaned forward. "They looked like trouble to me, but all they wanted was a shovel, some elk jerky and some rope. They talked in that sing-song voice, but I think they mentioned gold. Not enough of that around to spit on."

"Sammy is tall and dresses mostly in coolie clothes. He's very polite and speaks English well."

"They all look alike to me," Lulu said as she locked up the case. "Sounded as if they might be going to Smiley Creek. You know that's a rough area sometimes, although with the moonshiners pretty much wrapped up, it might be better now. Sure you don't want some protection now?"

Nellie considered. She remembered how terrible the Smiley Creek Lodge had been. With the moonshiners gone, it should be safer. "Later. If the Chinese men come back, see if you can get their names. Thanks, Lulu. I may stay up there all night, maybe at the Rocking O cattle ranch. I met Ben O'Donnell last fall, and he seemed nice enough."

Just over the top of the pass, Nellie stopped her auto and climbed out. She had had no trouble getting up the steep, unpaved road. As always, the Sawtooth Mountains awed her with their fierce peaks, their remoteness, and their bulk. She retrieved her camera, set it up on its tripod and took a photograph. A meadowlark's song rose from the depths below. Robins sang to each other. She decided the two Chinese must have been Sammy and one other.

Smiley Creek. Nellie remembered the signs for now-closed mines near the Smiley store the summer she had spent time with the Basque sheepherder Alphonso on the Fourth of July Creek and road. Sawtooth City was one. Obsidian another, but that was farther up the road. Vienna, abandoned years ago. She slowed her borrowed automobile and turned off the main road onto a side one. This one must be near Smiley Creek and would avoid the outpost where the moonshiners used to hang out. She did not want to take the chance of running into the possible remnants of them.

The road bumped along and up and down in long sweeps. Eventually grass grew in the middle meaning few autos or wagons now used the stretch. Finally, she came to an auto parked beside the trail. No one was in it. Pollen had turned the front windshield yellow. She didn't recognize it, but all autos looked much the same to her. She turned her auto around and parked across from the solitary machine and climbed out to investigate. Maybe there were some clues inside as to who owned it. She peered through a window but saw little as all the windows were smeared with yellow. There were an increasing number of evergreens as she had followed the road, but it didn't seem like enough to create such a fog. Maybe it had been there a while.

Nellie tried to open the door. It was locked. She tried every door—two front, two back and a rumble seat. The same. She gazed around to grassy meadows, rocky scapes, brush and trees. A few birds chirped, but she heard no sounds of people. The sun was rising toward noon. The rugged mountains still carried some snow and hung over her like ramparts. She decided to load her camera pack, take the lunch she brought, and follow the road by walking. Maybe she would find the owner of the empty auto. Or Sammy.

No animals appeared in the road and it soon degraded into a wide trail and then narrowed until it wasn't much more than an animal track, dusty and rocky. Flowers grew in abundance, reminding Nellie of her trek with Pearl up Fourth of July Creek about a year ago. So much had changed since then. Still, her photography remained the same in many ways. Being a crime photographer, though, had lessened her opportunities for her artistic photographs, as she liked to think of them. She stopped and looked back. She should have taken a photo of the yellow-smudged auto, but she hadn't even considered it. She would do it on her way back.

The trail divided. One looked hardly used and the other not only appeared to have been trampled on by a number of travelers, but it widened and wound through a stand of trees that shaded the way. It climbed a short, steep hill then leveled out. Soon, she heard the sound of water running. That must be Smiley Creek. The path wound through bushes, bigger rocks and more trees, making her way more difficult. On the opposite side of the creek, the hill steepened even more. Still, she heard and saw nothing but the water, as it tumbled over rocks and downed branches. As she walked, she noticed short paths from her trail to the creek's edge, some cleared of brush; others appeared to be temporary and soon to disappear. When she came upon a large, flat rock off to the side of the trail, she decided to rest, eat her lunch, and decide what to do. When she sat upon the rock, she could still see where she had traveled and where she would go. A breeze began ruffling the tree branches and cooled her down. Insects buzzed around her and she felt sleepy. It was then she heard voices. Not sure why, she slid down off the rock and hid behind it.

Three men ambled down the trail. One wore a full beard and scrunched hat so she couldn't see his face. The other two had dirty faces, one with a cowboy hat and the other bare-headed. The latter two were clearly not Chinese. The man without a hat appeared to have wet and greasy-looking hair, as if he had dunked his head in the creek. She immediately noticed a large knife in his leather belt, a knife with a black blade and large enough to be a machete. She decided to stay hidden.

Nellie heard bits and pieces of their words as they passed her. "…gold…" "…fools…" "Chink…" They didn't sound like people she wanted to tangle with. When she could no longer hear boots on the path or any voices, she raised her head an inch at a time. The trail was empty. She decided to continue on her way, go in the direction the men had come from. She hoped their auto would be gone when she returned. Back on the path, she had a grim foreboding for Sammy. Maybe seeking him out alone wasn't such a good idea.

"Stop it," Nellie told herself out loud. She was as good as a deputy to Charlie, the sheriff for whom she took photographs, and not so incidentally the man who wanted to marry her. A deputy would do his duty—search for a missing person. She would do the same. As she neared the water, she slowed, keeping her eyes on her surroundings, treading softly even in her boots. Behind a screen of brush, she spied what looked like a camp—a fire ring, strewn metal utensils, a canvas tarp that was torn and bundled. A wooden box lay broken on its side. This camp had been kicked to pieces. That was what those men had done.

She waited and crouched low to see if anyone was still around. Only the sound of falling water disturbed the peace of the forest. When a small, yellow bird landed on a middling tree next to her, she decided no one else would appear, and the bird thought Nellie herself was a part of the forest. She had settled onto the ground and began to push herself back up, when she saw brush move on the other side of the camp clearance. A man stood halfway and then fully rose. He had been waiting, just as Nellie did. She froze in place.

The man limped into the camp. He was Chinese, but not Sammy.

Chapter 2

THE MAN WORE A KNIT miner's hat that hugged his head. When he turned to look around the disheveled camp, a long black braid swung with him. By now, most Chinese had cut their braids, the better to fit into Western mode, although not all. Maybe he was new to the country. Nellie decided to chance meeting this lone Chinese, but she wanted it to look accidental. On hands and knees, she backed up along the path, trying not to dislodge rocks or branches. She hoped the river water would cover her sounds. Then she stood up to walk up the path, just as if she were first arriving. The man looked up, flinched as if to run, then probably realized she was a woman. His face relaxed, but not his stance.

"Hello," Nellie called. She walked into the camp. "What happened here?" She didn't even have a walking stick with her. "Do I know you?" A strange question, maybe, but the man made a motion with his head. Perhaps he understood her. "I am looking for Sammy Ah Kee. Do you know him? Have you seen him?" The ground, littered with dried rice and beans, troubled her. Why would someone do that?

At Sammy's name, the man's eyes narrowed. He glanced around as if looking for an escape route. He did not have a stick either, or any form of weapon that she could see. Still, he said nothing.

Nellie ventured further into the camp. The creek ran a dozen steps away, but it had pooled into a small lagoon with a bubbling white waterfall a dozen feet up the course. It would have been a pleasant campsite. "I saw men along the path. Did they do this?" She gestured, sweeping her arm back and forth. "Are you all right?"

Only then did she see the man's pant leg, ripped with what appeared to be blood stiffening the cloth. Inside the ragged edge there seemed to be a still-flowing wound above his knee. "Oh my. Your leg. Can I look at it? Do you have anything—?" She took a step nearer.

The man leaned over to set a box upright and he sat down, extending his leg. Nell knelt and pulled his pant leg away to study what looked to be a slashing wound, still suppurating. "Do you have a belt? We need to stop this bleeding." She held out her hand.

The man half stood and pulled a woven belt from around his waist. He did not wear coolie clothes like so many other Chinese. Instead, he sported torn Levis like a miner, and a blue shirt. His boots were heavy and worn, old and well-used. Up close, his face was sun-wrinkled, his hair turning gray at his temple. A sketchy growth of hair on his face sprouted in pepper and salt.

Nellie took the belt and wrapped it around his leg above the wound and tightened it. The blood stopped oozing. She glanced around the camp to see if there was anything to hold water and a cloth of some sort to wash the wound and bind it. A shallow gold pan lay turned upside down near the fire ring. She wished she had Charlie's pack. Sheriff Azgo always had just the right tool or cloth to fix anything. She saw no piece of material, so she opened her own pack and pulled out a large handkerchief, one of Charlie's she had intended to return to him.

"Hold still." Nellie picked up the pan and returned with creek water. She wet the kerchief, squeezed it and placed the cold cloth on the man's wound. He moaned but didn't move his leg. She felt strange touching the man's skin and leg—an intimate act she would not have done except for the wound. She released the belt and waited. No more fresh blood appeared, but the handkerchief was now stained a deep burgundy. Back at the creek, she swished the cloth around to rid it of blood. She wrung it as dry as she could and returned to wrap it around the wound, so deep she could see muscles, but she hoped not bone. "You need to see a doctor. That cut is too deep to leave as is. I have an auto and can take you to Stanley. Do you know anyone there?" She looked up into his eyes for the first time. They were black as obsidian and so deep, they didn't reflect light at all. "I am Nell Burns. Who are you?" She stood and moved back.

The man heaved himself up and took three steps to tower over Nellie. He smelled of the woods and a slight under aroma, maybe of incense mixed with sweat. She retreated another step and tripped on a piece of wood but managed to right herself. She thought briefly of turning and running, and then the man spoke. She recognized no word of what he said and she assumed it was Chinese. He motioned to himself and said three words.

"Joe?" Nellie asked. "That's your name?"

He repeated the words, which sounded to Nellie like Joe High Sing. Like Sammy, she understood many Chinese men adopted western names. Then he said, "Ner Bun."

That was close enough. "We need to find you a crutch to help you get to the auto." Nellie gestured to the path up which she had labored. Getting this man down to the trail and out seemed impossible. His leg must hurt and she didn't want the blood to run again. "I'll be back soon," Nell said. She motioned to his leg, picked up the piece of wood she had stumbled over and put it under her arm. "We need a stick, a crutch, for you. Sit and wait." She patted the box. "Rest your leg."

Nellie floundered around the campsite and the creekside. She found what she hoped would work—a long stick that might have held up the torn tarp. When she brought it back to Joe, she again gestured putting it under her arm and taking two steps. It was too long for her but should work for him. He stood and tried the stick as a crutch. Nell nodded but realized it needed padding to be of any use. Again, she looked around. The tarp. It could be folded up under Joe's arm.

At last, they set out down the path and reached the trail out of the woods. After a while, the man managed the crutch more easily, and they were able to hike along in a steady rhythm. At the rock where Nell had rested, she motioned to the man to rest while she checked on the gash on his leg. It still looked painful but had only bled a small amount more. She was hungry and tired and had failed in her search for Sammy Ah Kee. She had no idea if there was a doctor in Stanley, but surely someone would know what to do with the leg.

From a distance, Nellie finally saw her automobile. It sat alone in the field where she had left it. She heaved a sigh of relief, and some of the tension dropped from her shoulders. Up close, nothing looked amiss on the outside or on the inside. She opened the passenger door and helped Joe sit down. The space for his legs was cramped, and he moaned once before she closed the door. Around on her side, she slung her pack into the back, climbed in the front, and managed to get the motor running with little effort, and soon, they bumped along the dirt road.

Mid-afternoon turned sunny, but dark clouds hovered on the northern horizon. The sun shone on the Sawtooth Mountains that scraped the sky. Nell was tempted to turn into the cattle ranch but decided to continue into Stanley. There would be people at the saloon/café. If nothing else, perhaps the owner would help the two of them. He had been helpful to her when she was taking photographs a year ago. She had sent him a copy of the railroad brochure that showed his place of business.

In Stanley, at the café, Nellie opened the entry door so Joe could hobble in. She followed.

"Hey, get that Chink out of here!"

The voice came from near the bar where cowboys were hunkered down, just as they had been on her first visit the summer before. She ignored it and helped Joe sit at a table, maybe the same one where she and Cable O'Donnell, the cattle rancher, had sat with Gwynn Campbell, the sheep owner. It seemed much longer ago than a year. Cigarette smoke hovered in the room, mixing with a yeasty smell that was surely beer. The barkeep and owner sauntered over. As he neared, his face lit up.

"Goldurn, it's the picture lady! Thanks for the photo piece from the railroad. I hung it up behind the bar." He nodded and stuck out his hand. Nell took it and he almost shook her arm off. "What are you doing here this year? Still camping out with those Baskos?"

Nellie smiled up at him. "No, I'm looking for someone and found this man with a deep gash in his leg. Is there a doctor of some kind in town?" She remembered his name was Sam. Unfortunate. She must only say "Sammy" for her friend.

The barkeep frowned. "Might could be a vet who would know what to do. No sawbones around here, except by chance sometimes." He turned and studied the men at the bar. In a lowered voice, he added, "Them men don't like Chinese, but he can stay until we figger this out. I've got a side room where I serve

19

Chinamen and colored people when they're about." He jerked his thumb toward a door leading into a smaller, darker space and a few tables. "He can wait in there."

Nellie saw a person sitting at a table, his head on his arms in front of him. A tall empty glass sat in front of him.

Joe limped toward the room, as if he were used to such treatment. At the entrance, he stopped, let out a roar and lunged toward the one other person there. In a loud clatter, Joe upset the man and his chair so they tumbled to the floor and the man sprawled and groaned. His attacker jumped on him, lifted his arm and swung it toward his victim's head.

"Stop! Stop!" Nellie shouted and rushed forward. She grabbed Joe's arm with both of her hands and hung on. "This is Sammy! He's the man I've been looking for. What are you doing?"

By then the barkeep intervened to pull the two men apart. "Hey! No fighting in here. Take it outside like normal men!" He used his strength to release Sammy and helped him to his feet.

Sammy stared at Nell. "What are you doing here?"

Joe yelled. "This man murder Hung Lui! I saw him. Get sheriff!" Those were more words than Nellie had yet heard from him, and in English.

The patrons from the bar had crowded around the door, jeering and calling. Sam the barkeep's action had pushed Nell to one side, but she hustled back to Sammy's side. The chaos of the moment subsided and mounting silence overtook everyone.

"I did not kill Hung Lui. I found him in the river. Maybe you did it!" His voice keened at the end. He jabbed his fisted hand at Joe and would have jumped at him if the barkeep hadn't restrained him.

Loud exclamations from the doorway erupted. "Two chinks. Fight! Fight!" "Kill 'em all!" "My bet is on the big one!"

Nellie stepped between the two Chinese, her back to Sammy. She turned to the barkeep. "Can you get them away from there?" She gestured to the men in the doorway. "I'll try to settle these two down. I know there must be a mistake. Sammy wouldn't hurt anyone."

The barkeep did as she requested. He stepped to the doorway. "Free beer for everyone. Back to the bar!" The men immediately turned around and were herded like sheep. The saloon keeper winked at Nellie. She mouthed a thank you.

"Sammy, please set the chair upright and sit down. Joe, you sit down on the other side." They, too, followed directions. "Now, Sammy, we have all been worried about you." Mentioning his mother probably wasn't a good idea in this rough place. "What happened?"

The thin Chinese man pulled a still sodden piece of paper from his chest pocket. "Map. Hung Lui…We followed… Fell asleep… In river…" He spread it out, but most of the printing had disappeared. Once again, he hung his head. Nellie feared he would begin to cry.

"Slow down, Sammy. Begin at the beginning."

Sammy took a deep breath and let it out. He nodded. "Hung Lui and I bought map. He said we would find gold, lots of gold. We bought gold pans, picks, and, and, equip—."

Nellie nodded to encourage him. The other man sat in silence, his face almost etched in stone. She didn't know how much more English he had, but he didn't interrupt. He probably understood the gist of what Sammy was saying.

"Traveled to Smi-ley Creek." He said the name slowly. "We hiked and found other men who looked for gold, too." He lifted his arm and pointed at Joe. "He was there and saw us go by." Joe grunted.

"Hung Lui said we go higher up. Get away from crowd and find our own gold." He stopped and wiped his face.

Just then, the barkeep came into the room with three glasses of beer and set them down in the middle of the table. "Guess you three could use a little mouth wetting, too." He turned abruptly and left.

Sammy eagerly grabbed one and drank half in one long swallow. Joe followed suit. Nellie wasn't sure a lady would drink a beer in a saloon with two men, but she picked up the last one and sipped carefully. The cold and wet liquid seemed a godsend. She motioned to Sammy. "Please continue."

"I went first and climbed up higher. I stopped to rest and fell asleep." Sammy lowered his head, as if in shame. "I woke up and saw sun moved. No Hung Lui. I hurried down steep trail and back to find him. He was nowhere. At last, I found spot where men panned." Again, he pointed to the other man. "They all gone. Funny lump in water, so I waded out. It was Hung Lui. His throat was cut. River cleaned it out. Head almost gone." And then, as if he had held his sorrow in until that moment, Sammy did cry in great retching sobs.

*　*　*

Sammy kept his head down on the table. Under his arm, he glanced toward Nellie Burns to see if she would send the others away. Nellie Burns is a white girl. What would she know about heartbreak? Seeing Hung Lui with his head nearly cut off, his neck screaming at him as if he really were, as if Sammy had been there to save his friend and had not. Hung and Sammy played cards, talked about how they were lucky to get to Idaho, how they almost messed up in Canada at the border. The kind of territory they crawled through there was so much like the grasses and trees and bushes around Smiley Creek, they might have been sneaking in again as they followed the map. But this time, Sammy got in and Hung didn't.

Who did this? There's Joe High Sing, claiming Sammy killed Hung, but he never would. They were partners in crime and then looking for gold, something the white people didn't want the Chinese to have—safety in Idaho or gold.

Maybe Joe did it. He was panning for gold. Sammy saw Joe but didn't know if Hung had seen him. He's a big man, hard to miss with that long braid. Hung and Sammy were modern. They didn't want anyone to think they had just arrived so they cut their braids. His mama screamed at him, saying he wouldn't go to the ancestors with his papa or her when they died. Didn't he have any respect for their ancestors? She cried and cried so Sammy said he would grow his back. But he had not. Hung and Sammy cut each other's hair, keeping it short, but a little longer so Sammy's mama would think they were growing their braids back. Maybe this is why Hung's throat was slit. The ancestors want retribution. Or maybe the tong from Twin Falls seeks Chinese-not-Chinese, the ones with no braids. Joe might know, but he thinks Sammy is a murderer. No talking to Joe.

Maybe Nellie Burns has suffered heartbreak. She told Sammy's mother and Sammy that she lost her father in a bar fight. She had to identify him. Maybe that was heartbreak. When Sammy stole his father's body from the ice store with the one-eyed miner, Rosy, he said he had suffered heartbreak when the flower lady died with a growth in her chest. Sammy's father said so. The miner tried to kill himself with drink. He did not succeed. He should have used a knife. All Chinese know how to use knives. Hung Lui died at the hands of a Chinese. A white man would have used a gun and shot Hung Lui in the head.

Sammy took Hung Lui into the woods. He can return Hung's bones to China when the time is right. Hung Lui would want to go home. He has family in Guangdong—a sister, a mother, a father, and a baby brother. They are poor. Everyone in Guangdong is poor. That is why they all want to come to Gold Mountain—*Melica*, as Hung called it. He and Hung thought they would find gold in Gold Mountain so they bought the map. With gold, Sammy could take proper care of his mother. She had saved dollars from Sammy's father's sale of herbs and spices. His mother continued to sell these things, but she did not have the proper knowledge and she and Sammy were running out of savings.

After Sammy left Hung, he went to the camp where the other Chinese lived. He knew it was theirs because he saw an altar in it. He knocked everything apart. Whether they killed Hung Lui or white men did, no one saved him.

What if white men killed all the Celestials there on the river and only Hung Lui was in sight? Sammy should have looked more. Maybe he carried blame on his soul, too.

It was time to send his father's bones back to Guangdong, Mother said. No, it was too early. He would not yet be bones. Sammy would not dig him up until two years had passed. Then, maybe. They should have left him out in the open for birds and animals and insects. Then, he would be ready. And where would they send the bones? Elder Sister was gone. Little Sister—where was she? They had never heard. Mother wept. She ground and boiled. So few Chinese left in this Idaho Gold Mountain, few bought her goods. White girls who were in a family way, they

24

called it, wanted herbs to take away the family. Mother knew how to stop that. Someday, a man would stop her. Joe could try to kill Sammy, but he did not see a knife. Joe may have one hidden. A knife slashed his leg. Maybe he did that to himself when he cut Hung's throat. Sammy does not trust him. He might even hurt Miss Burns. She had been kind and Sammy's language was much better because she taught him. Miss Burns had not interfered with his mother, and his mother and he saved her from pneumonia. Sammy's heart had been broken many times. But it continued to beat. He would do what his ancestors wanted.

His mother would be ashamed to see or hear Sammy cry. Chinese must be strong, she said. Stoic. Brave.

Chapter 3

NELLIE PUZZLED OVER WHAT TO do. She wanted to put her arm around Sammy but did not think that was wise in this place—not with Joe standing over her, and the barkeep and the men in the other room waiting for a fight outside. For them, watching two Chinese men fighting was like watching roosters attacking each other, drawing blood, and hoping one would kill the other. The sooner she could leave Stanley, the better. She could put Sammy in the front seat and have Joe stretch out in the back seat and take him to a doctor in Ketchum or Hailey. But she did not trust him.

Sam the barkeep stepped into the backroom. "I sent word to the veterinary to come here to see to that man's leg. Not sure he will when he learns it is a Chink, er Chinaman. Guess one animal is same as another as far as a knife slash goes."

Nellie closed her eyes briefly and kept her mouth shut. Pouncing on the saloon/café owner wasn't going to help the situation. This backroom seemed to be getting darker. There was one window to the outside, but it was covered with a shade, perhaps even a rug, it was so thick. She wanted to lift it, let sun in. Maybe Joe and Sammy would calm down. She wondered if Hung Lui and Sammy Ah Kee had driven an automobile up to Smiley Creek. If they did, where was it? And whose auto would it have been?

She remembered Sammy had borrowed the boot-maker's auto in the past but doubted if he would have let Sammy take it over Galena on a useless venture, that is, if Sammy had been honest about where they were going. She had only seen the one auto that was covered in pine pollen—nothing else. The men she saw took it away, she assumed. The two Chinese men might have hidden an auto anywhere. The long drive in gave them lots of places to hide it to keep it safe.

Sammy's wails wound down. Then he gathered more steam and his cries became louder. She had never seen a man sobbing. Her father had cried in his cups sometimes, but not like this. She wanted Sammy to stop. The men would come back and make fun of him, perhaps a dangerous situation.

"Sammy, come with me. I'll take you back to Hailey. Your mother wants you." Oh dear, that was the wrong thing to say. He had lifted his head briefly and then lowered it again, groaning. At least that was quieter.

Joe sat at another table, his leg resting on a wooden chair. Undoubtedly, the slash was hurting him, possibly throbbing with pain. She wished she had some of Mrs. Ah Kee's opium to give him, but that would put him to sleep. While she dithered about what to do, standing and then sitting again, a man came through the front door and then crossed to the room where she and the Chinese were huddled. At last, maybe some help.

"Are you the vet?"

The man nodded. "Who is hurt? I heard one of the Celestials had his throat cut." He looked around. "Obviously not one of these two." He chuckled at his own joke.

"Joe here. His leg has been slashed. I managed to get the blood stopped and get him here. I think the cut needs to be sewed up."

"Heh, heh. Are you a doc?" He stood, not making a move toward Joe.

"No, of course not, but I've had a similar slash in the past—on my arm. It was sewed up and healed just fine."

The man came closer to Nellie. He smelled of garlic, anesthetic, and tobacco. His blondish hair was unkempt and his clothes fit like a scarecrow's. Nellie would have backed up if she had been standing. She was glad she didn't have a wound.

"I remember you." The man smiled, seemingly pleased with himself. "You're that picture lady who caused all the trouble around here last summer. You at it again?" He walked back to the doorway and looked back and forth into the main room. "Nope, don't see no dead people in there."

"Would you please look at this man's leg?"

"I don't normally take care of people," the vet said. "Especially not Chinamen. We run most of them off around here."

"If you fix him up, he can leave," Nellie said. "That would appear to make everyone happy." Except the Chinese man in question and her if she had to take him back in her car. Sammy quieted. He still sat slumped, but his eyes took in what was going on around him. His wrinkled forehead made him look deep as if speculating about Joe. She sensed Sammy didn't trust the big man, either.

When the vet finally stepped over to Joe, the big Chinese held up his hands. "I not *animar*." He waved back and forth in front of himself. "No touch." He lifted his bandana-ed leg up and placed it on the floor under the table.

The vet shrugged. "Makes no difference to me. I heard you were hurt bad. If this little lady stopped the blood, she probably saved your life." He gestured to Nellie. "Mostly, she kills people. You're a lucky one." Sammy, Joe, and the vet all stared at Nellie.

28

She rolled her eyes. It wasn't as if she were really a murderer.

Nellie stood and walked over to Joe. "Give me your leg."

Joe moved his leg out to where she stood.

"Now, place it on that chair so this doctor can see the slash and maybe sew it up. It will hurt, but you look like a brave man. Stop acting like a child." She turned to Sammy. "Go find a piece of wood he can bite into. That will help. I know what I am talking about."

Joe lifted his leg with his arms and replaced it on the chair. Sammy hurried into the big room to the fireplace and found a piece of kindling. He brought it back and handed it to Joe. "She is right. This will help." He looked as if he would touch Joe's shoulder, but he did not. Instead, he laid the small piece of wood on the table.

"Now you," she said, motioning the vet to come closer. "I put this bandana around the wound. I'll take it off and you see what you can do with the slash. I saw muscle, but not bone. It could be our trip to my auto caused more damage—he had to hop with a branch for a crutch quite a ways."

The barkeep came to the door of the room and motioned to Nellie. He whispered in her ear: "Does anyone need a ride back to Ketchum? Should I report what happened up Smiley Creek to the sheriff?"

"I have an auto and I can take Sammy Ah Kee back. Joe High Sing is another matter. Would you be willing to take him? I'm afraid to have them both in my automobile while I am driving. And I can report to Sheriff Azgo. Whatever happened, it was in Blaine County, his jurisdiction." When she told Charlie about her day, she could also include the three men who talked about "Chinks" as they headed down the path past her, and about the camp she had seen thrown into chaos. There was an explanation from Sammy about that event. It was clear to her there had been other Chinese on Smiley Creek. What had happened to them? She had heard of massacres of Chinese men in mining areas, but mostly those had happened quite a while ago. Once the mining had ended in the Wood River Valley and in the Stanley Basin, most Chinese had left. No one needed their laundry services or restaurants anymore. Ah Kee had been the only supposed doctor in the area. Without him, people he had treated had gone too. She didn't think Mrs. Ah Kee had really taken his place as an herbalist, although she tried.

She turned to look back in the room where the vet leaned over Joe's leg. Sammy leaned, too, to get a look at the wound, she supposed. Joe groaned, but the stick of wood was in his mouth. The vet most likely was sewing up the slash. Joe's face was ashen, and he held onto the arms of the chair with both hands, his knuckles whitened. She faced the barkeep again. "I don't think he will feel much like traveling today, and I want to return my auto. Is there a place where Joe could spend the night and then hitch a ride tomorrow back south?"

*   *   *

Nellie and Sammy rode in her automobile, and Joe would return to Ketchum with the barkeep in the morning. The vet had given him some laudanum after he finished sewing up the slash—a workmanlike job, in Nellie's opinion. He charged $5 and Nellie paid him, saying Joe could pay her back later. She wanted to leave because she had another search in mind, one she kept to herself. She needed gasoline, so she drove to the combination livery stable and gasoline pump near the turnoff from the highway into Stanley. Fortunately, it was open. Once again, she paid as Sammy said he had no money. He had found no gold on his foray. When he looked as if he might begin crying again, Nellie hurried to assure him: "The sheriff will reimburse me as this has now become county business." She gestured back to the café, encompassing Joe in her thoughts.

"All right, Sammy, you can see I have finally learned to drive an automobile after your first lessons to me last year, I still have difficulty with the gear shift from time to time, but I am much smoother." She smiled at him, hoping to calm him down from all the trauma. Sammy grimaced, and Nellie took it for a smile back. One step forward. "I want to drive back toward Smiley Creek and have you tell me exactly what happened with you and Hung Lui and Joe, too." His face crumpled again. One step back. Too soon, maybe.

Even so, Nellie turned toward Smiley Creek just before the lodge onto a rough dirt road, one that had seen heavy use because no grass grew in the center. Meadows filled with lush grasses and colorful wildflowers accompanied their way until they reached stands of timber. The road climbed and eventually, she saw the creek below a steep bank. She rolled down her window and heard the rushing water. Spring runoff muddied the swift-moving creek. How would the men have panned for gold here? She stopped the auto and climbed out, waving Sammy to join her. "How did you pan for gold in here? It looks much too fast, dangerous even."

"No, no." He pointed south. "Up that way. Much calmer. Better water." He gestured with his head. "I will show you." Back in the auto, Sammy pointed up the road. Nellie engaged first gear, jerking the car a little to her embarrassment, and continued on their way. The road leveled out and they arrived at a crossroads. "Go that way," Sammy said, gesturing to the left.

"What is the other way?"

"Sheep camp. Old town of Vienna." He shrugged his shoulders. "Ghost town." He grinned this time. "Spooky. I can show you."

"Not this trip, Sammy. I want to go back to where you and Hung began your trek up stream, where you saw the other gold panners." Sammy mumbled. "What?" she asked.

"More ghosts. Unlucky. Spirits of Celestials haunt here now. We should go back to main road and go to Ketchum. This is not a good place."

"Ghosts of the gold panners?" A shiver ran down Nellie's back as she thought of what happened to Hung Lui and Joe's bloody slash on his leg. Maybe this wasn't such a good idea. It might be better to bring the sheriff back. He always scolded her for going out on her own. Still, she wasn't alone. Sammy was with her and she knew he was a strong man with wide shoulders and muscular arms. She could only bring Charlie here if she knew the exact places to search.

"Mmmmm," Sammy hummed. "Down this road, I can show you, maybe. We did not come this way."

"How did you get here? An automobile? Who drove? Where is the auto? I didn't see it when I traveled the other road into the creek. Only—" No need to go into the three men she saw. Sammy might declare them to be ghosts as they were white men.

"Someone stole it." Sammy looked ready to cry again. "After I left Hung Lui, I went to find the auto, one we borrowed. It was gone. Tong took it! Bad men!" This time, his face screwed up in anger. "Tong expelled my honored father. Tong leader died because my honored father could not save him." His words spilled out, contrary to his usually calm speech. "Tong lie, say honored father poisoned him with herbs and compounds. Lie!"

Nellie wasn't certain how to respond. She had heard of tongs from Rosy and Charlie, the groups of Chinese men in Boise and elsewhere. She thought of them as men's clubs rather like the Mormon men's groups in Hailey. Or, if not clubs, then bible studies and religious groups to which women were not invited, not that she would want to attend. It was just another example of how women were treated—slaves in their own households, unwanted outside the home except in women's groups. So, it was true for Chinese women as well. No surprise there.

When their automobile crossed a rough bridge, Sammy said: "Leave auto here. We will walk that way." This time, he pointed upriver. Here, the water had calmed and eddied into small inlets where it circled and pushed against the creek bank. River might be a better descriptor, there was so much water. She aimed her auto toward a flat spot of low grass, as if someone else had done the same thing, and they both climbed out. Nellie took care to lock the doors and the boot, after she extracted her camera pack. She might as well take a photograph or two. They might prove helpful if she and the sheriff returned, with or without Sammy.

The split skirt Nellie wore nowadays enabled her to follow Sammy along a rough trail without stumbling too much. Lulu, the storekeeper at Galena Lodge, had mentioned them to her and found a pair her size. She no longer had to wear men's pants, a welcome relief, as they always bagged too much for comfort. The only disadvantage was that she now looked female and sometimes it was important to appear to be a man, as it had been in the mine in North Idaho. Just thinking of her experiences there caused a shudder. Maybe there were ghosts in this place—all kinds.

Not far along, Sammy stopped and pointed to the water. "Here. Men panned for gold. I saw one I knew—Joe. He is a member of

Boise tong. He saw me, too. Hung and I kept walking to begin our hunt for gold. Our map said secret place marked with 'x' farther up the river." Sammy's voice slowed as he talked. "Maybe we were wrong, and this was the 'x.'" He squatted down to put his hand in the water, swirling it around, lifting up mud from the bottom and holding it. He smelled it and dropped it back into the water. "Need my pan."

"Could you tell if the men here had found any gold?" The current ran slowly in this spot, so she wondered how it would wash over the gold pans, as she understood was needed to find gold in water. She had seen how large hoses had sluiced over piles of dirt near the ghost towns of Custer and Bonanza, farther north above Stanley. No mining took place there anymore either, although a few people still lived in the area. There were so many vacated mining towns and camps in the whole area—Blaine County and Custer County—it was a wonder there weren't ghost conventions. She decided not to mention her thoughts to Sammy. He believed in ghosts. Between her driving lessons and his English lessons, they had talked about some of his religious beliefs which entailed spirits in many guises. While Sammy dug his hand into several places in the river mud, she wandered a few steps back and forth, trying to see any clues of how men had worked there. Many trees grew near the shoreline. High above, she saw large birds circling, hawks, she thought. A robin sang in the few aspens behind them.

"Where was the camp you destroyed?" It must be the one Nellie had seen when she found Joe with his slashed leg.

"Back there. Down river."

"Was it Joe's camp?"

Sammy stood up. "No, different place. Joe's camp is there." He looked toward the woods behind them. "You saw it? You found Joe? No one else?"

Nellie shook her head. "It was torn apart, too. Joe hid. He and I stood up at the same time. I thought it might hold bad men." Again, she decided not to mention the three men she had seen, not sure why. Maybe because it would disturb Sammy too much. "Show me where you and Hung Lui headed upriver and where you stopped. Can you estimate how far along you were? How much time it took to go and then come back?" Photos could help her estimate distance and maybe time.

After Sammy washed off his hands, carefully inspecting them first, they began hiking along the creek. The trail meandered more like a deer track, narrow and only partially packed down. The grasses along the creek bed waved in the water as it sloshed up the sides. Near the edges, the mud seemed deeper and more widespread. Eventually, it cleared, and the rocky bottom gleamed in the afternoon's sun's rays.

At last, Sammy stopped. "Here." He circled his hands. "I fall down, fell. I decided to wait for Hung Lui because I could not hear him." He stepped toward a small glen of trees. "I sit and wait. I sleep. Sun moved off me and onto water."

Nellie decided to set up her camera and take a photo. Not only was the place quite beautiful, it epitomized many of the forested glens along the Wood River farther south. No wonder Sam had napped. She felt as if she could lie down and do the same, listening to the murmuring creek, the slight breeze in a few cottonwood trees higher up, their shiny leaves turned to the sun. And yet, a possible massacre had taken place just downriver. She shook her head and concentrated on setting up the photograph.

"Did you pan for gold while you waited?" She covered her

head with the black cloth. Such a peaceful, lovely view.

"No." Sammy sounded sad. He had lowered himself against one of the trees near a large rock.

When Nellie removed the black cloth and picked up her film holder to insert it in the camera and take out the black slide, she glanced at Sammy. "Why not? It seems the perfect spot."

His face grew long. "I did not know how. Hung Lui had not shown me."

Nellie pushed the shutter release. Now she had her photo.

"Can I take a photograph of you?"

"No! Only take dead people's photos. As you did with my honored father." Sammy stood up from where he had lounged. "We should destroy all of your photos of my father. They might keep his spirit caged, unable to return to China."

"I am not sure your mother would agree. She wanted the photograph I took, so I printed one for her." Sheriff Azgo also had a print in his file of the investigation of Ah Kee's death. It seemed an age ago. "Where to next? Where is Hung Lui buried?"

Sammy appeared reluctant to leave the sunny, warm place by the river. Nellie surmised no one had died there. Still, the sun was lowering. It was time to head back to the automobile and maybe the camp Sammy said he had destroyed. "Sammy, I need as much information as possible so the sheriff can begin to find your friend's murderer. Please help me. And help Hung Lui."

The Chinese man stared at Nellie. "Why do you want to help? He is just another Chinaman. No one in Idaho wants the Chinese here. No one in *Melica* wants Chinese."

Nellie was surprised Sammy used the name many Chinese used for America, being unable to pronounce the "r" in their language. "I know. I don't know why. Some people think the

Chinese take jobs away from the locals. I suppose, too, because you have a different culture than most Americans. But it is important not to let a murderer get away. He, or she I suppose it could be, might do it again. We want the Chinese to be treated fairly. At least I do, and I am sure Sheriff Azgo does as well. He is sworn to uphold the law. Killing a man, even a Chinese man, is against the law." She stepped to Sammy and touched his shoulder. "Please, let us go."

After another glance around the forest glen, the creek, and the trees, Sammy heaved a sigh along with his shoulders. "All right. We can leave."

They walked back along the trail they had followed to get back to the spot where the men had panned for gold. "Sammy, were all the men Chinese?"

"I am not sure. They all wore hats and clothes that mostly looked like coolie clothes—you know the kind of clothes when I act as servant to my honored mother." His forehead wrinkled and he stared at the ground. "I have tried to see them as they were. One might have worn other clothes, a shirt and vest, but that does not mean he was not Celestial." He waved his hand down his front. "These are American clothes I wear now."

Indeed, he did wear woven black pants and a white cotton shirt stained with sweat and dirt. Still, to Nellie's mind, he looked Chinese even if his head had not been covered. Ah, his head. He wore a rounded, flat hat—a Chinese hat. "Did they all wear hats like yours?"

Again, Sammy thought. He studied the water for a while. "No. One wore a straw-type hat. He was not the one with western clothes—a different man. Joe must have known the men he panned with. Ask him."

"All right. If I ever see him again. Where is the camp you said you ruined?"

"Ruined? What is that?"

"Tore up. Destroyed. You said you went to a camp and broke it up. You said it was back there." Nellie pointed to the wooded area they had passed earlier, on the way from her auto. Late afternoon clouds formed, and the hawks were gone. "You said it had an altar and that was why you knew it was Chinese." She turned in a circle. "I don't understand. Were there two camps? Was one for white men and one for Chinese? And if so, then Joe must have been at the one for white men. Is that how things work out here?"

Her friend nodded. "That is how things work, as you say." Sammy began to walk down the larger path, headed back to their automobile. "Hung Lui and I were going to camp by ourselves. We didn't want to be around other prospectors. No one is honest. They jump on each other. They jump on claims. That is what we learned from the man with the map. Keep it secret, he said." Tears sprang to his eyes. "Mother was right. We were… fools, she called us." He squinted his eyes tighter and scowled. "Hung Lui and I believed. Ghosts are more real than the gold he promised us."

Nellie and Sammy stood in silence. And then Nellie heard voices. They were still a ways away, but were getting closer, coming from the same direction as her parked auto. "I hear something," she whispered. "We must hide. It could be the white men looking for more Chinese." She pushed at Sammy. "Back into the woods and down!"

"White men?"

"Shhhh! Hurry!" She led the way into a clump of thick cottonwood trunks. "Come!" Shrubs slowed her down, but she knew they could hide behind them.

Sammy stood by a tree trunk. "Just more sucker gold panners. More Chinese with 'secret map.'"

"Can you see them?" Nellie knelt and then lowered herself further. "Down, Sam!"

Sammy sat down next to Nellie and folded his knees in front of himself. "Who else would come to pan gold? I am not afraid of Chinese like you are." He grinned at her.

A man's voice called. "He ain't there now, Hank. Musta floated downriver. Probably in the Salmon and headed to tarnation."

Another man mumbled in a bass voice, his words indistinguishable. Nellie pulled Sammy's head lower. "Not Chinese," she whispered in his ear.

"Then whose automobile is that parked near the bridge?" That was the first man. "Same one we saw earlier."

"Mebbe someone following us."

"Except they got to this place before us." His low voice carried well in the trees.

Nellie risked lifting her head to see if she knew the men. She ducked swiftly. The two along the river were the same ones she had seen earlier when she hid behind the large rock, the ones talking about Chinks. Their conversation then and now seemed to confirm that they were responsible for the damage and maybe murder of the Chinese men, or at least Hung Lui. She wondered if Joe had seen them as well and escaped.

Bass Voice called from farther upriver, from the direction Nellie and Sam had just come down. "Maybe he wasn't dead. Maybe he pretended he was and then he took himself out of the crick and ran away."

Nellie looked a question at Sam. Could that be true?

Sammy shook his head, moving the grass around him.

"What's over there?" First Man said. "I saw the grasses moving."

"Just a snake. Let's get out of here. If we came back to save a Chink, we ain't got one to save no more. Either he up and ran or he floated down to the Salmon. They ain't worth nothin' anyway."

"I tell you, that man was the best laundry coolie in the county. I hate to see him gone."

The voices moved away. Nellie lifted her head and saw backs going down the path again. As she had done with the earlier camp, she waited and cautioned Sammy with her hand, taking hold of his arm, so he would not stand up. "Wait," she whispered low.

Her caution paid off. First Man came back up the trail and looked around. He walked to the water, picked up a branch, and swirled it in the creek. He shook his head, then stepped over to the grass and brush, close to where Nellie and Sam hid. He pounded the ground with the branch. "Damn snakes." Then he dropped the branch and hurried after Bass Voice.

After another wait, Nellie sat up. Sammy did, too. "Now what?" he asked.

Nellie shook her head. "I don't know. First, it sounded as if they were the ones who murdered Hung Lui. Then it sounded as if they were looking to help him, although that seems most unlikely." She turned to Sammy. "What do you think?"

"I have never seen these men before. They did not pan gold with the men I did see, although with their hats and leaned over panning, I did not see much." He looked both ways on the trail. "I think we should go over Galena and leave the gold behind." This time he stood and offered a hand to help Nellie up.

"All right. You were going to show me where you buried Hung Lui. Is it near here?" She too glanced around. The creek continued down the slope, on its way to the Salmon, as the men had pointed out. "I am worried about my automobile. What if they try to steal it?" She did not want to end up having to hitchhike over the pass back to the Big Wood River Valley. She could just hear Charlie or Rosy or both laughing at her failure. And Henry the miner who owned the auto would be unhappy for certain. She took a deep breath. At least she did find Sammy Ah Kee and could return him to his mother. Joe, the other prospector, would surely turn up again in Ketchum or Hailey, either to charge Sammy with the sheriff or to try to beat him up again.

Sammy began the walk down the creek to the bridge. "You follow. If we meet up again with those men, you hide."

Nellie followed, but she had no intention of hiding if they did run into the men. Her presence might save Sammy from being beat up or worse. They took their time, both reluctant to run into anyone. Her automobile was still where she had left it parked on the grassy stretch. She circled it. There appeared to be no damage or anyone having tried to mar it in any way. She opened the boot and slung her camera pack in. One photo was all she had taken. That was hardly worth the effort. It was so pretty here that she might come back. Charlie would want to see where Sammy had seen the men and find out if there were more dead bodies. She felt a chill on the back of her neck. Nellie turned around, thinking someone might be watching them, but no one appeared. She opened both front doors. "Sam, get in. Let's go. I don't like this place." She noticed he had turned as pale as her neck felt. Maybe he had a premonition, too.

Chapter 4

WHILE NELLIE DROVE, SAM AH Kee slumped toward his window. Soon, Nellie heard him snoring, a gentle sound. No wonder, she thought. All the trauma and finding his friend with his throat cut. She concentrated on driving her borrowed automobile, knowing it would take a couple of hours to get back to Ketchum.

Nellie could not stop thinking about her engagement to Charlie Asteguigoiri, the sheriff of Blaine County, her boss. Second thoughts, indeed third and fourth thoughts leapt to her at odd times. She had said yes to being Charlie's wife. But being a wife was something she had never wanted in the first place. Or did she?

She felt like a pendulum on a big grandfather clock, like the one her grandparents had wound in their living room. Every quarter hour, it struck a series of notes. At the first quarter hour, it was short. At the half hour, it was longer. At the third quarter hour, longer still. At the hour, the clock not only played a series of notes, it bonged the number to match the hour. Nellie's thoughts went from short to medium to long to bongs. She wished she had someone to talk to and not just Charlie. She didn't want to hurt his feelings if it sounded as if she were wavering. She wasn't.

Or at least, she didn't think so. She just wanted to sort out her feelings from her most deeply held principles. She had already warned him she would keep photographing, ideally for him as sheriff, but also for herself as independent photographer—portraitist, landscape-ist, whatever appealed to her-ist. She was not going to spend all her time cleaning house, cooking, shopping (not that she had much money to spend, but she'd seen women shopping and shopping without a dollar in their pockets). She had things to do, places to go. What would Charlie think if she wanted to travel to Boise or Spokane or even Seattle, or maybe up to Canada, or even farther—to Chicago—all by herself?

It wasn't as if Nellie hadn't heard Charlie say she needed a keeper. What would he ever think about her driving up to Stanley Basin by herself to find Sammy Ah Kee?

A keeper was the last thing she wanted. She wanted to share a professional life with Charlie, as deputy, as photographer, as investigator, even as an open ear to listen, brainstorm, whatever. Women could do that, probably better than men friends or colleagues. Did Charlie and Rosy talk about the work they did? Rosy seemed to enjoy the tasks Charlie set out for him, even though they used to spar a lot. Their unusual relationship over Matthew probably had something to do with that. Matthew didn't look at all like Charlie, his real father, except through the eyes. Even his hair was on the brown-blondish tone, not black at all. And yet, Matthew's eyes were dark like pools of water at night. Charlie's eyes. Nellie could get lost in Charlie's eyes—dive in, feel secure and wanted and loved. Or, they could be like pieces of obsidian—cold, indifferent, almost cruel.

Maybe Charlie could help clean, cook, and whatever needed doing. Share the chores. Nellie harrumphed to herself. She doubted it. That meant they would have to hire help. She had read in the Boise newspaper at the library in Hailey that people in Boise hired Chinese boys or men to cook, clean, and serve as houseboys. It was clear the newspaper thought only rich households could do that. What, then, did the women in those households do? Shop? Go out for lunch? Play card games? Her own mother had worked hard and also did cooking and cleaning until Nellie was old enough to help out, not that she spent much time being a helpmate. And when she did, she did a slap-dash job, as her mother pointed out. Her mother. How long since she'd had a letter or even written one herself? That was what she needed, a mother to talk with. They had never been particularly close, probably because her mother worked so hard and was always tired. Should she go to Chicago? No, her mother should come to Ketchum and Hailey. Meet Charlie. Listen to Nellie dither. She had been good at that in the past. Goldie usually had an extra bedroom or two and Nellie could pay for her mother to stay a couple of weeks. When? As Sammy slept and Nellie drove, keeping watch for animals crossing the road, she composed a letter in her head.

> *My dear mother,*
>
> *It has been a long time since I've written. My life is topsy-turvy now that I am a police photographer. I told you about that, didn't I? I work for Charlie Asteguigoiri, Sheriff Azgo, we call him. His last name is impossible. He is Basque. You have probably never heard that word. It refers to an area in Spain, actually Spain and France, but he is from the Spanish part. All Basque speak their own language, filled with "x"es and lots of vowels. No one knows where it came from.*
>
> *We spent several weeks in North Idaho on an assignment from the U.S. Marshall for the area, who*

seems to think Charlie can handle all the tough problems having to do with bootlegging and moonshining. I know few officials in Chicago even bother. The mob has taken over there. But here, it is still a crime to ignore Prohibition. At any rate, Charlie and I traveled by train to Spokane and then on to Bitterroot, a mining town in the panhandle. You can find it on a map. We had less success there than in the Stanley Basin, but we did solve some problems, survived a landslide, a mining disaster, a fire, and came back to Ketchum. Or at least, I did. Charlie lives in Hailey. I still live with Goldie Bock in her boarding house.

It turns out I am engaged to Charlie. I never thought that would happen. I have made it clear that I will continue to photograph, both for him as sheriff, and for my own dreams. I know I told you I had two photographs in an art museum in San Francisco. Both sold, which gave me some money of my own, as did my photography for the railroad.

Would you come visit me? I think you would like Charlie and I want you to meet him. We are getting married, but we still don't have a date. I love you and miss you and wish you were here to talk to. I can buy a train ticket for you. Please let me know.

Your loving daughter, Nellie

She went over her proposed letter in her mind. That should do it. Maybe her mother would come and maybe she would not come. When she thought of her mother, she remembered perfume, carnations, a warm heart, a smiling face, beautiful hands. She loved her, but she forgot that from time to time. Nellie needed her mother now.

*   *   *

Nellie stopped at the boarding house in Ketchum to let Goldie know she was back in town and would return after she dropped off Sammy Ah Kee at his mother's house in Hailey. By now, Sammy was awake, but he mostly sat with his head turned to the view out his window.

Just as they neared Hailey, Sammy spoke. "What will my mother say? I know she was correct in her thinking. I am embarrassed." His "r"s sounded more like "l"s, a sign he was tired and not using his learned consonants that he and Nellie had worked on during his English lessons. Or tired of trying to sound American.

"She was so worried about you, Sammy. Mothers can forgive." Nellie had no idea if Mrs. Ah Kee would forgive her son for disappearing as he had done. The woman could sound like a drama queen one moment and then hush her tones into a soft patois the next. Her face often had no other expression than stony.

When Nellie drove her automobile into the woods to Sam's mother's place along the Big Wood River on the edge of Hailey, Mrs. Ah Kee opened the door. When she saw her son, she scowled. "Where have you been? I have been so worried about you. Shame on you for making me worry." Nellie had expected Sam's mother would have been delighted to see her son. She should have known better. The Chinese woman never seemed happy about anything.

"Now, we go dig up your father. We must return his bones. It is time."

Sammy hung his head, whether in shame or disagreement,

Nellie didn't know.

"Mrs. Ah Kee, I am certainly not an expert, but I don't think your husband's body, er, his bones, er, …." She didn't know how to say the body might not yet be bones. She was certain a year was not long enough, especially if he had been buried in a coffin. "Um, where is he?" Nellie rather doubted there had been a funeral and burial at the Hailey cemetery, but she hadn't ever thought about it. She just knew that Ah Kee's body had been stolen from the morgue at the hospital and never returned. She had even taken a photograph of it at the behest of this woman and her son. She still had a negative. She found herself looking around the shaded cabin where the two of them lived and wondered if the herbal doctor's ghost hid somewhere nearby. Then she shook herself. No ghosts.

"Come," Mrs. Ah Kee said. She grabbed Sammy's arm and pulled him toward her and then pushed him along a path that led toward a forest copse that appeared to Nellie to be too thick to even walk though. She followed. Surprising to Nellie, the path kept going, as if it had been used frequently, and seemed to continue toward Bellevue. Nellie calculated that they walked between the river on one side and a forest of aspen and cottonwood and smaller evergreens on the other. The cottonwood trunks shot up straight and narrow, the bark thick and dark gray with branches sprouting higher than Sammy's head. Mrs. Ah Kee walked quickly. She looked like a gnome beside her son and the tall trees, slightly hunched but determined. The sound of the river dimmed and then grew louder and dimmed again as the river twisted and turned along its way below Della Mountain.

Who had carried Ah Kee's body all this way along the narrow path? It must have been Sam and his mother, or maybe a few other members of the Chinese community, although she thought most of them had left. There were more Chinese in earlier years than Nellie had known about, certainly counting Hung Lui, Joe, and others who panned for gold up in the Stanley Basin. There were still old mines around Hailey and Bellevue, but they were gone by the turn of the century, according to Rosy, except for the Triumph Mine up the east side of the valley. At the Triumph, the men mined underground for lead and silver, not gold. She almost bumped into Sammy who had stopped next to his mother, who gazed around herself.

It was evening when Nellie and Sam had arrived. Even in early summer, though, the woods felt dark and almost threatening. It was then she noticed a nearly full moon rising in the East, its soft glow peeking through overhead branches above the tall hills of the valley. Nellie remembered photographing the moon shadows out at Last Chance Ranch, long before she knew anyone except Rosy. That seemed eons ago, but it had just been a little over a year.

"Here," Mrs. Ah Kee said. She stepped off the path and walked deeper into the woods, away from the river. "There." She pointed to a mossy glade and stepped into it.

The bird song had stopped. There was a deep silence, now that the three of them stood still. Even the rushing river sound had disappeared. A quiet, serene resting place for the man who had doctored with herbs and potions up and down the valley and had been known as Doc Kee. Nellie bent her head, and the aroma of pine, aspen leaves, dark soil and moss assailed her senses. Why not leave him here? The moon edged higher.

"Ahhh!" Mrs. Ah Kee shrieked. She hurried to one edge of the glen. "He is gone! He is gone!" Sammy and Nellie both rushed to her side. Heaps of dirt surrounded a shallow grave that had been hidden among the white tree trunks of the aspen. Indeed, those trunks almost appeared to be bones standing tall around the grave, as if in homage. It reminded Nellie of the aspens around Lily's grave, Rosy's wife, near Last Chance Ranch.

Sammy moaned. He slipped to his knees and buried his hands in the dirt. "Who did this?" He eyed his mother beside him.

She shrieked again and covered her face. Her shoulders heaved up and down and she appeared to be sobbing. "My husband, my husband. He is gone!"

"Honored mother. What have you done with my father? His spirit will never rest after his body has been treated in this manner."

For several long moments, Mrs. Ah Kee sobbed and keened. At last, she removed her hands from her face, which in the moonlight was dry and wrinkled, an old crone. She thrust her shoulders back and faced her son, her head held high. "How would he turn to bones if he were buried in dirt? How could you return his bones to Guangdong as you must do, if he stayed in the dark underground? No decent son would let him founder in the soil, his soul wandering forever in this desolate land!" Her voice climbed higher with each accusation. "Your greed led you away. You left to hunt for gold!" She spat the words, her spray landing on her own chest.

Nellie wished she were anywhere but here. She didn't know what to do—try to calm Mrs. Ah Kee or flee the once-sacred gravesite and let the two of them resolve what to do. She felt sorry for Sammy, who had now lost a friend and his father's body and was being blamed for both. Moon shadows lengthened around the three of them, but the forest seemed blacker than ever. A magpie honked in the distance, reminding her that she should find the sheriff and tell him about the events near Smiley Creek. She shuddered and had turned toward the entrance to the no-longer quiet glen. Mrs. Ah Kee's whine changed its tone.

"Your father is buried as he should have been—open to the sky." She strode to Nellie's side and took her arm in what felt like a claw. "Come. Now we will see if his bones are ready. The animals and birds should have performed their sacred duty, as my son did not." She pulled Nellie along just as she had pulled Sammy along earlier. They moved deeper into the woods and Nellie found herself stumbling over salal, fallen trunks and branches, barely able to keep her balance.

"Mrs. Ah Kee. Stop it! I will fall. Let go!" She jerked her arm, but the elderly woman kept what felt like a death's grip on her upper arm. "Sammy, make her stop!" But Sammy was nowhere to be seen.

Chapter 5

SAMMY'S MOTHER, OPAL AH KEE, would do anything to get her way. She wanted Sammy's father's bones gone. Sammy didn't know why. And yet, against their custom, she wanted Sammy to bury his father in the woods. Sammy did so, asking his father's pardon with each shovelful of dirt. No one knew what they did. Only his mother and Sammy knew. Sammy did not dig up his father.

Sammy's mother left him in China and she followed Ah Kee to Gold Mountain. They said they would send money. No money came. Sammy and his sisters begged food and clothes. Elder Sister and Little Sister and Sammy lived in a chicken pen. Even chickens would not live in it. An uncle, a family friend and not a blood relative, sold Elder Sister into a marriage in Shanghai. He bought food. Sammy worked for him, slopping pigs, slaying chickens for market. He caught bats and sold those, too. Nothing saved Little Sister. Uncle sold her and Sammy ran away, wanting to find her. She was gone.

Hung Lui, a friend who lived near the chicken pen, ran with Sammy to Shanghai. They found work on a ship going to the new world. The ship captain chained them to the deck where they scrubbed wood and painted. The chains were rusty. Hung and Sammy scraped and scraped the rust. When they docked to unload the cargo, Hung and Sammy escaped. But they were not in Gold Mountain. They were in Canada.

Sammy could not let his mother imprison Miss Burns. Why she wanted a white woman to be with her, he did not know. As much as Sammy hated to go back, he did. Standing up to his mother was not what an obedient son would do, but he did. Sammy imagined his father telling Sammy what he must do. "Let her go," Sammy said.

Miss Burns, her face a pale flower, pulled her arm away and scrambled to Sammy. Did his mother turn her into a ghost? No, Sammy felt Miss Burns cling to him. She shivered and her hand grabbed his arm. "We will go. Honored mother, stay here." Sammy's voice came from a deep place, like his father's when he was alive. Mother shrank, almost as if she were the ghost, but she was not. She screamed at Sammy, saying Chinese words he did not remember.

Sammy led Miss Burns back through the woods to the Ah Kee house. "Do you want tea?" The moon still shone down on them.

"No, Sammy. I—I want to leave." She stood straight and looked up at him. "I am sorry. I must go." She brushed a piece of grass from her hair.

"You go home. These are Chinese doings. Forget them." Sammy held out his hand, maybe to shake hers and bid her good-bye. "I go to my mother, my honored mother. I will take care of her."

Miss Burns walked to her automobile, opened the door, climbed in. Her face was as white as the moonlight. Maybe Sammy would never see her again. She climbed out again. "Sammy, I must tell the sheriff."

"Do what you must, Miss Burns. You go now. I go now. You are not Chinese. You go." Sammy bowed to her. He was sorry he ever came to Gold Mountain. And now the ghost of Hung Lui wanders, alone and lost.

Chapter 6

NELLIE FOUND CHARLIE AT HIS home in Hailey. Rosy and the boys, who had lived in Charlie's house to go to school in Hailey, had moved to Last Chance Ranch, along with Rosy's sister, for the summer. With school out, they could roam free. Rosy motored back and forth to Ketchum to help the sheriff.

She knew she was in a state when she knocked on his door late at night. She had to tell him all that had happened. She couldn't hold it in—it was all too terrible. She knew she was being weak-kneed, something she despised. Maybe Charlie would see what a spineless creature she was and change his mind about marrying her. It didn't matter. She needed him. She needed his matter-of-factness. She needed to stop believing in ghosts and gods and bones and cut throats.

Charlie answered the door, and it was evident that he had been asleep. His hair was askew with more gray showing than when it was combed. He wore a robe, hanging loosely without a tie. His eyebrows lifted and he said nothing. Nellie stared as at a specter. What was she going to say?

"I—I—a dead man. Bones. Missing." She felt tears begin to gather in her eyes. "I—I need your help."

He moved aside and motioned for Nellie to enter the house. "This is news. Are you hurt?" He closed the door behind her.

"Where is Moonshine?" Charlie took her arm and guided her to a chair to sit down. "Wait." He moved toward the kitchen, and while she sat down, she heard a cupboard door open and close. "Here." He came back to her side and knelt, handing her a fragile glass with dark brown liquid in it. "Drink. You clearly need something."

Nellie sipped what turned out to be brandy. The warmth slid down her throat and eased her distraught sense of the world spinning and turning upside down. A fleeting thought—no wonder people wanted alcohol.

Charlie waited for Nell to calm down. At last, she sat back, the chair's arms enfolding her. "I have so much to tell you. I don't know where to start."

"How about with the dead man?" Charlie said.

"Yes," Nell lowered her head. She began with the visit from Mrs. Ah Kee, the drive to Smiley Creek, Joe High Sing, the café in Stanley, Sammy's story of Hung Lui. Somewhere in that recital, she finished the glass of brandy—medicinal alcohol. Charlie said nothing the whole time. He watched her, his facial expression barely moving, but he held her hand. Such warmth and comfort, Nellie thought. "There's more," she said.

"Go on, unless you are too tired. I should let Goldie know you are safe. She did telephone, afraid the Chinese had sold you into white slavery."

"All right." She waved her hand. "Do that."

The next thing Nellie knew, sun streamed in a window onto her face, where it lay on a pillow, and a cozy blanket curled around her shoulders and neck in a bunkbed. She smelled toast and bacon. She lifted the blanket and saw she was still dressed but her jacket and pack sat on a table nearby. Her shoes were tucked neatly below the bed. She wiggled her toes inside her socks. She wondered where she had left off with her story.

In the kitchen, she found Charlie drinking a cup of coffee. When he saw her, his eyes smiled and so did his lips. "You look like a normal person this morning. How do you feel?" He stood up and lifted a kettle from the stove. "Tea?"

"Yes, please. I'm sorry, Charlie. I didn't mean to stay all night." She sat down at a place set for her. "I am starving. Can you feed a hungry lost soul?" She hung her head.

"The price will be the rest of the story. I assume there is more." Charlie filled a plate with toast, bacon, and a scrambled egg.

It all smelled so good, Nellie felt like crying. Maybe she wasn't back to normal yet. Instead, she stood and circled Charlie with her arms. He held her, too.

"You'll be all right now," he whispered. "Eat."

*　*　*

Three days later, Sheriff Azgo steered his automobile up and down the swales on the way to Smiley Creek. Nellie rode beside him, "shotgun" as Rosy described it, with Moonshine in the backseat. Charlie's auto handled the dirt road much better than the auto Nellie used to go the same distance a few days before.

"We're not in a hurry, are we?" She turned to study the man. His dark good looks always surprised her. She wondered why. Maybe she expected the stern visage and frown most photographs or drawings of western sheriffs posed. He wore a half-smile today and she knew he was humoring her, at least somewhat, in this possibly wild goose chase to find answers to the mystery Sam Ah Kee had posed about the gold panners. Who murdered Hung Lui? And where were the other Chinese?

"No. You are the director today." He glanced over at her and then back to the road ahead, rutted and washboarded, as if many autos traveled it. No one else was on the road that day.

"There is an old mining town—Vienna. I'd like to see it. Sammy Ah Kee said ghosts lived there. I wondered what he meant by that. Maybe some of the Chinese who left Hailey moved out there." The Smiley Creek road must have been busy years ago when the towns of Vienna and Sawtooth City grew up around the gold found in both places. By now, the towns were empty and, she thought, they should have been almost overgrown and disappearing. Hence the ghosts.

Charlie nodded. "You are in charge. Just tell me where to go." He geared down to drive around deep ruts.

"Hmmm. Someone or several ones drove on this road during the spring thaw. It's a mess." They had passed beyond the small bridge over Smiley Creek and headed west as Sammy had described the way to Vienna. As they continued, Nellie spotted dozens of white animals streaming down from a hillside onto a meadow. "Look! Sheep. Hundreds of them. I didn't know this was sheep country, too."

The sheriff slowed the car to a crawl. "Maybe the cowboys scared them out of the Fourth of July area. I did not know this either, and I am sheriff of this county. I wonder whose sheep they are." They both watched for a while, as sheep dogs kept the ewes in line, along with their lambs. Every now and then a black sheep appeared in the mass of white wool. The dogs bounded back and forth. Finally, a sheepherder on horseback appeared at the crest of the small hill. He looked picturesque in his brimmed hat and long chaps.

"Do you suppose that is Alphonso, the sheepherder I stayed

with last summer for a while? He does look familiar." Nellie opened the automobile door and walked around the front, trying to get a better look. "Let's go towards that hill," she called to Charlie. "I'll walk to catch up." Two dogs made a beeline towards her. "Oops. No, I'll ride with you." She dashed back to climb into the automobile. Sheepdogs did not like strangers around their charges. Nellie looked back to the end of the meadow they had passed without really noticing it. A sheep camp sheltered near the line of evergreens, where another dog lounged.

The horseback rider angled to meet them on the road. As he drew near, he waved his sombrero type hat and shouted. "Miss Burns! Sheriff!" A grin split his sun-tanned face and his white teeth gleamed.

"It is Alphonso!" Again, Nellie climbed out to greet her friend. "Keep Moonshine in the back," she ordered Charlie. "The sheepdogs won't like him at all!" She heard her dog making sounds to get out as well, but she didn't think it was safe. Nellie bridged the barrow pit beside the road and hurried over to Alphonso. She grabbed his hand as he leaned to greet her. "Alphonso! How are you! And what are you doing in this backcountry? Whose sheep are these?"

"*Hola*, Missy! It is good to see you!" He grabbed her hand. "And the sheriff, too!" Then he slid down from the horse to shake Charlie's hand. "You chase moonshiners again?" He laughed and shook his head. "No, how you say it? You scare them last summer! They vamoosed or gone to hoosegow."

Nellie noted his English was much better, but his accent deep. He had learned much in the past year.

Alphonso held the reins in one hand and shooed the dogs off with his hat. "Go back." He whistled and the dogs ran off. "I work for Mr. Campbell." He pointed to the sheep camp. "Same old camp and camp tender. That old dog survived last year. I like him for company." He gestured toward the animals who had obeyed his whistle. "Different dogs this summer. More coyotes this summer, but these dogs *bueno*."

"Good to see you, too, Alphonso," Charlie said. "I wondered if you would be with the sheep again this year. Gwynn is not up to his old self. He broke a hip this spring. I wonder who is taking care of the ranch and all the sheep. Do you know?"

Alphonso looked back and forth at Nellie and Charlie. He leaned forward, as if to impart a secret. "No good times for Señor Campbell, I think. New foreman, Señor Alvido, not the best." He closed his mouth and shook his head. "I say no more," he added at last.

"Alphonso, your English is so much better," Nellie said. "Of course, we won't say anything if you think we should not. But perhaps we could visit Gwynn and see what is going on." She wanted to assure him that they would not talk out of turn or get him in trouble. "Where did you spend the winter?"

"In Hailey," he said. "I found work. I miss the sheep. Outdoors for me in summer." Again, he grinned. "Are you hunger? I make mutton stew for you."

"We were on our way to Vienna to see what is still there. Have you seen it, and is anyone living in the remains?" Nellie liked the idea of mutton stew, especially the way Alphonso prepared it.

"Specifically," Charlie added, "we are looking for some missing Chinese men. Have you seen any in your area this summer? They might have been panning for gold." Charlie shaded his eyes from the sun but kept his attention on the sheepherder. "Any other Basque in the crew this summer?" he asked.

"Vienna abandoned. Ghosts there now. A few men, too, but buildings?" Alphonso twisted his hand back and forth. "Fall down. Men not dress like Chinee that I have seen." Alphonso put a foot in the horse's stirrup.

Nellie hurried to respond about the stew. "Thank you, Alphonso. We will continue up this road. Don't prepare stew for us today, as we also must search along Smiley Creek. We think some men were hurt or killed while panning for gold. Have you heard anything?"

The sheepherder swung up onto his horse. "No, only camp tender from Hailey. He knows nothing about anything." He talked down to Nellie and Charlie. "Good to see you. Thank you for help last summer. *Gracias. Adios.* Come again." He turned his horse and rode toward the sheep.

"That stew sure sounded good," Charlie said.

"Yes, I thought so, too." Nellie sighed. Business first. "Let's motor along to Vienna. Maybe the non-Chinese men I saw came from there. Both Sammy and Alphonso have referred to ghosts up there. Do you know anything about the old mining town?"

"Yes. It once supported some two hundred buildings—stores, saloons, a boarding house, even laundries. That is a possible Chinese connection. Was not Hung Lui a laundryman?" Charlie escorted Nellie back to her side of the automobile and returned to settle in behind the driving wheel.

"He may have bought the map from someone in Vienna, I suppose. Still, if it is only a ghost town now, who would that be? Was it gold the miners were after in the area or lead and silver like the Triumph mine north of Hailey?"

There was so much to learn about the Wood River Valley and the Stanley Basin—their histories went back over many, many years. "I wonder if anyone found their dream mine and struck it rich." Nellie watched the trees and brush go by.

"Some men did, but they left with their riches, I would imagine. Now it is the sheep ranch owners who make money, but I do not think business is good for them either. With mining almost gone and sheep ranching difficult, maybe Ketchum will disappear entirely. It used to have many more people than it now does." Charlie glanced at Nellie again. "We would have better luck finding a house for us in Hailey."

Nellie wanted to let that statement pass. She still wasn't ready to talk nuts and bolts about a married life. But maybe she should. "I suppose so. Opening a studio in Hailey might bring me more customers than I ever get in Ketchum, but I like the old-fashioned air around Ketchum. Hailey seems to bustle too much." She touched Charlie's shoulder with a hand. "Still, that is where your main office is, so that should be where we settle down." But, she thought, he did come to Ketchum often, so she could do some portraits there and have her darkroom in Hailey.

Chapter 7

THE MEADOW WAS LOST BEHIND them as they continued on the road to Vienna. Soon, they were in trees again and the road smoothed out somewhat. After what seemed like miles and miles because of the winding road and again, many ruts, they came upon a cleared area where tumbled-down cabins and a two-story log building with a wide porch sinking into the ground told them they had reached Vienna. "What an odd name to use here in the backwoods of Idaho," Nellie said. "Do you suppose some of the miners were from Austria?"

Charlie parked his automobile alongside the road near the wood building. "I think this must have been a boarding house," he said. "Do you hear anything? I thought I did when I first turned off the motor." He walked toward the dilapidated structure and Nellie followed him.

"No. Let's listen." They stood quietly for several minutes, not moving. To Nellie, the place seemed completely deserted with no sign of life at all. She inhaled deeply. The aromas of sun on dust, sagebrush, and old logs hung in the air. Logs lay hither and thither and a few old buildings lined what was once a street. At last, a bird sang, a melodious robin, she thought. From the corner of her eye, she saw a black-tailed squirrel dash down one tree and over to another.

"What are you doing here?" The voice came from behind, and both almost jumped, not expecting anyone else to be there.

Nellie turned and responded first. "Hello. Who are you? Do you live here? We had heard this was a ghost town and I wanted to see what it looked like. I even heard there were ghosts."

The man was as tall as Charlie, but pot-bellied and bearded. He looked as if there were few shower facilities around, as his clothes were wrinkled and dusty. His pepper and salt hair stood half on end and he rubbed his hand through it, mussing it even more. He spat tobacco sideways out of his mouth. "Heh, heh. That's what they say about all old mining towns." His laugh sounded like a creak from a long unoiled door opening. His voice was low, and she immediately thought of the men that she and Sammy had hid from along Smiley Creek. He wore a short-sleeved shirt that once was maybe underwear cut off at the elbow. His arms sported thick graying hair and not much muscle.

"Any mining going on still?" Charlie asked. "Silver and gold, was it not, at one time? That looks like a broken-down stamp-mill over there by the creek." His eyes had taken on the hard-as-granite look that Nellie had seen in them several times in the past.

A small nod from the man gave the answer. He turned back to Nellie. "Want to see some ghosts? That old saloon down the way offers some up."

"I don't know. Are they frightening?" Nellie wasn't sure she wanted to accompany this man anywhere, but Charlie spoke up again. "We do. Do you want to show us around? Care if we bring our dog? He has not been out of the auto for a while."

Not waiting for an answer, Charlie opened the back door, and Moonshine jumped out. He circled the three people, found a place to relieve himself in a patch of grass and came back to stand by

Nellie. "Good dog," she murmured and fondled an ear. His black fur felt warm from being in the auto. She could feel it through her divided skirt and was comforted. She knew Moonie would protect her even if there were ghosts. But then, so would Charlie.

"There's some feral dogs and cats around. Better keep him on a rope," the man said.

"I'm Nellie Burns. This is Charlie Azgo. What is your name?" She rubbed Moonshine's neck and then looked up at the man. He was studying her.

"Bubba." He didn't offer any more and she didn't ask again. He turned and walked up what was once probably a street for the thriving mining town, but now a grassed-in path. "The old mine is up thataway," he said and gestured up the road that continued on. "It's all closed up."

No one else seemed to be around, but Nellie imagined the sounds of children playing, women carrying laundry with their long skirts swishing as they walked, wagons lumbering along filled with ore or gold. Long ago, people worked and lived there in the broken-down log cabins, bought groceries nearby in what were now shacks leaning from weather and abandonment. They neared what Bubba said was the saloon, and she could almost feel a piano playing and men laughing. Maybe Sammy was right. She was hearing the ghosts of a prosperous mining town filled with men, women, and children. All gone.

"This here was a saloon," Bubba said. He swept his arm toward the forest. "Quite a few of 'em in fact. Not many women in those days so there weren't no churches." He laughed the creaky sound. There was no door, so Bubba stepped in and Nellie and Charlie followed. A few tables with chairs, broken into pieces and lying on the floor, proved people, men, had frequented the place in days when liquor was sold everywhere. "Up the way is an assay office, leastwise, that was what it was. There's still a weighing machine, but it ain't no good anymore. No gold on it."

"Were you here when Vienna was in its heyday?" Nellie thought he might be old enough, but she didn't want to insult him.

"Hell, no. I ain't that old!" Creaky laugh. "I might look old to you, but I was just a kid in those days. My pa worked the mill up here, and me and my ma lived in Stanley in the summertime and I was sent down to Ketchum for school in the winter. I like being around these old buildings, though. Ma said it was too rough here for kids and women. Even for boys like me." He walked over to what might have been a bar. "Wish I'da seen more than I did. I just got to come up once with my pa, and that was when most of the miners had left. A few men still come up and pan for gold in the crick, but most always, it's empty." He pointed toward the back. "There was a old piano over there." He hummed a little ditty, but Nellie couldn't place it. "See any ghosts, Miss?"

Charlie poked around, but Nellie wasn't sure the floor would hold all of them up, so she stayed in place by the door. "It does feel as if a piano might be playing sad songs," she said. "Do you live here now? Are you lonely?"

"Nah, I don't get lonely. I don't stay up here all the time. I just like to hang around, especially in the summer. Do a little panning myself from time to time. I find enough gold to keep me going. In the winter it's too cold and the road is closed."

"Who do you think made all the ruts? It looks as if there might be a lot of traffic up here, especially in the spring before the mud has dried." Charlie disappeared through another door. Nellie wished she had followed him.

"Hell of a mess, ain't it? Sheep camps, goldpanners thinkin' they'll find a fortune." He shrugged his shoulders and moved closer to Nellie. Moonshine did not take that kindly and uttered a low growl. Bubba moved away again.

"Wanna see the assay office?" The disheveled man stepped outside, just as Charlie returned from wherever he had explored.

"I would," Charlie said. Nellie looked at him in exasperation. They weren't going to find anything in this dusty and broken-down old mining town, except the remains of buildings and furniture. She wanted to go back to Smiley Creek and see if they could find Hung Lui's grave. Sammy had given her some vague directions.

The three of them strolled back toward where Charlie had parked. It was a nice day with birds singing and a few white clouds drifting in the sky. Moonie moved off to chase an animal but soon was back by Nellie's side. Nellie no longer had the sense of ghosts and relaxed to enjoy the summer day. Bubba turned toward them and pointed to a shack that leaned to an alarming degree. It didn't look safe to enter, so they gathered at the doorway.

"It doesn't seem like much," Nellie said. "This is where the gold and silver were weighed and found valuable or not?" A large scale still sat on a leaning countertop, but it also leaned, so that one side appeared to be heavily laden with nuggets and yet nothing waited on the weighing surface. Another ghost? she wondered.

"This here place was one of the more successful mining towns," Bubba said. He had a wistful look on his face, what could be seen above his beard. His eyes looked shiny, almost as if he would shed a tear.

"Have you seen any Chinese people around here?" Charlie asked.

Nellie felt as if he had broken the spell. Bubba's expression changed. His lip curled and he slapped the leaning doorway. No tears lingered and none spilled.

"You mean those illegals from China? All the laws say they ain't supposed to come here and they can't own any property. If they show up here, I chase 'em out and tell 'em I'm gonna report 'em. They skedaddle pretty fast." He turned and almost knocked Charlie over as he pushed toward the once street. "Is that why you're here? You're looking for the Chinese?"

"No," Nellie said. "I have a Chinese friend who said we should see Vienna, the old mining town. That it still had ghosts." She emphasized the word "friend." She had a bad feeling about this ghost town. Moonshine stayed so close to her, she thought he did, too. She leaned over to pet him. He made his odd "arp, arp" sound, something he only made when he was disturbed. "Thank you for showing us around, Mr. Bubba. We'll stroll a little longer and you can go back to…" She didn't know how to finish the sentence. He hadn't appeared to be doing anything when he snuck up on Charlie and herself. "…whatever you were doing."

"I ain't doing much. I can show you some more buildings, if'n you want." Bubba seemed determined to stay with them.

Charlie shrugged, glancing down at Nellie as if to ask what more she wanted from their visit. Nellie didn't know, but she didn't want to leave yet. As Bubba walked down the road a ways, she leaned into Moonshine. "Can you find them?" She wasn't certain what "them" was, and maybe it was more ghosts. Moonie seemed to understand. He followed Bubba a few steps, and then headed off toward an old building that Nellie had seen when they drove in. Beside it were gold stamping machines, all rusted and with grass growing around where they settled in the ground. She knew this equipment from the rusted remains at Custer, north of Stanley, which she had visited a while ago. It was much less a ghost town than this one. People still lived near there.

"Hey, where's that dog going? Keep him with you!" Bubba called back to Nellie. "That dog needs to be leashed. It'll crap all over the place." He lumbered a few steps after Moonshine and then stopped. Moonshine had discovered something as he began to bark and turned in a circle near what appeared to be a closed doorway.

His barking did not disguise the noise coming from inside the mill—a shout of voices, real ones this time. Not ghosts. Charlie and Nellie hurried to follow Moonshine and they passed Bubba.

"Stop! Stop I tell you!"

Nellie saw that Bubba had drawn a revolver from somewhere, maybe from under his shirt. He must have been carrying it all along.

Charlie did stop, and he had his own revolver in his hand. "Drop that or I will shoot. I am the sheriff in this county. Drop it." He pulled his jacket aside to show his sheriff's star, something he rarely used to intimidate people. "Drop it." His voice never shouted as did Bubba's, but it was deadly sounding anyway—a rattlesnake's rattle to Nellie's ears. Bubba must have had the same impression, as he did drop his revolver and then turned tail and ran up the old road. Soon, he appeared again, driving an old Model T and heading down the road leading into Vienna and quickly through it. A cloud of dust followed him.

The shouts inside the mill had quieted some. Charlie reached the door and grasped the handle. It was locked. He looked around for another door or a window, but found nothing, nor did Nellie. Finally, Charlie lifted his leg and used his foot to pound on the door. It gave way with only a few stomps. Three Chinese men stood inside and lifted their arms, as if Charlie were holding his revolver on them. All together, they chattered in a language Nellie could only describe as Chinese. She could not understand a word, and Charlie didn't seem to, either.

With a slow motion, the sheriff put his gun away under his arm where it had rested in a holster out of sight. The men lowered their arms, apparently understanding that he did not pose a threat to them. "Do any of you speak American?"

"*Melican?*" one asked, then shook his head. Another put his hand in the air. "Some, some," he said.

"How long have you been held?" Charlie reached out to grab the man's hand and helped him over the split door. "Have you had water? Food?"

He shook his head and the others followed suit. Nellie wondered where she could find water for them. Only the river. "I'll find something for water and bring it back," she said to the sheriff. "We have the remains of our picnic in the auto. Why don't you get that and split it up while I get the water. Maybe Bubba brought some with him. He must have been in charge of keeping these men as prisoners, or at least seeing they survived. Maybe they were intended to be slaves." She hurried back to their automobile and opened the boot. There was a bucket there, of course. Charlie never went anywhere without being fully prepared to meet nearly any hardship. Moonshine accompanied her. "Let's go to the river," Nellie said. She rushed across the road, past trees and down a slope to fill the bucket and get it back to the three men who waited with the sheriff.

Food. What else could they find to eat? Fish in the river, but she doubted even Charlie was equipped for that. She certainly wasn't, and besides it would take a fire to cook fish even if they could catch them. She placed the bucket on the ground and motioned to take water with their hands. The men were polite to each other and pointed to the oldest to go first. He squatted and dipped a hand into the water, slurping it down in eager motions. Then he stood and a second man followed suit, and then the third. Charlie had picked up their few scraps from the picnic and offered pieces to the men. He snooped around to see if he could find more food anywhere in the structure outside of the space where the men had been held captive.

"Do you know Sammy Ah Kee?" Nellie asked. Maybe they would recognize the Chinese name. The men shrugged, almost as one. "Joe High Sing?" She tried a second time. The older man looked at the other two. He nodded.

"Joe High Sing. Fish. Run." His words were difficult for Nellie to understand, but she gathered that much.

Nellie pointed to herself. "Nellie." Then she pointed to Charlie as he came back to the group. "Charlie." She didn't know what they would do with the Ls. "What are your names?"

Again, they looked at each other. The older man placed his hand on his own chest and said words Nell could not understand.

"Do you know Hung Lui?" This time, the men frowned and grimaced. One took his finger and slashed across his throat. "Hung Lui dead."

Chapter 8

THE SHERIFF AND NELLIE PACKED the three Chinese men into the rear of their automobile. Nellie wondered about whether the men were trustworthy or would try to get out of the auto and run away. Charlie gave her a look when she tried to express her worry in whispers to him. Moonie climbed below the front passenger seat where Nellie sat. They began the long trek back down the road from Vienna.

"Could we at least stop at the place where Sammy found Hung Lui and see if they can tell us anything?" Nell pushed Charlie so she could help Sammy rebut Joe High Sing's accusation. She had developed and printed the photo she had taken when she and her Chinese companion had rested at the gold panning location and she pulled it from her pack. At least she had confirmation that Hung Lui had died, so Sammy had not been wrong about the dead man.

Nell turned to try and face the men. "Who killed Hung Lui?" She also used her finger to slash across her throat, feeling as if she were treading on her own grave.

All three men shook their heads, the oldest man the slowest to do so. "No. No. No kill Hung Lui," he said, his voice raising with each word. "White man." He said something to his companions, and they each nodded.

She passed the photo to the older man. "Do you recognize this place?"

He studied the picture, and finally, nodded his head. "Pan for gold. White men make us. They want gold." He looked about to spit at the back window but stopped himself. "We slaves. Find gold? They get. Bad, bad men."

Charlie drove and said nothing. When they reached the grassy stretch where Nellie and Sammy had parked her auto, he pulled off the road and stopped. "Let us walk up the river." He opened his door, climbed out and then helped two of the men to get out, too. Nellie did the same for her side. Moonshine tilted his head at the Chinese men but did not bark or challenge any of them. They moved as a small pack across the rickety bridge and up the river to where the creek added its flow. Then Charlie turned to the men.

"What happened here?" His deeper voice seemed to instill something different in the Chinese than had Nellie's questions.

The three men talked in Chinese, back and forth, nodding and shaking their heads. Again, the oldest man acted as spokesman with his rudimentary English. "We pan gold here." He gestured to the trees behind them. "We camp there." He pointed toward a different spot in the trees. "White men camp. Joe High Sing come. White men shove in water. Tell him to work." He pointed to himself and the other two men. "We Chinese-not-Chinese." He demonstrated by rubbing the back of his head. "No braids."

Nell remembered Joe's long braid. "Does that make Joe High Sing more Chinese than the three of you?"

"Old fashion. Not *Melican*." Then he turned and motioned from down the slope to up the slope. "Hung Lui and man come along here. They watch but not stop." With his hand, he motioned back and forth. "Hung Lui come back alone. He want to pan for gold here. I warn him. Not good. Go away. White men come back and order us out of water. Hung Lui shake his head." He waited to see if any of the other men added anything. "Joe come out, run up trail and maybe hide. White man follow but come back without Joe."

"What happened to Hung Lui?" Charlie asked.

"White man go in water, grab Hung Lui and cut." This man made the slashing motion again across his own throat. "No can help." He shrugged his shoulders. No one spoke for a long moment.

"What about our friend Sammy Ah Kee?"

"He not come back. Joe not come back. Maybe they meet each other." He pointed again to the three of them. "White men take us up road and lock us in building. We there many nights." He stopped talking.

Charlie looked at Nellie. She wasn't sure what else to ask and whether the Chinese men could be any further help. She remembered how distraught Sammy had been over Hung Lui's death. "Did you all know Hung Lui? Was he a friend of yours?"

Again, the men consulted in their own language. The same man answered again. "Hung Lui good laundryman. We know him." He shrugged his shoulders. "Sorry he killed." He hung his head, as did the others.

"Where do you three want to go?" Charlie stepped back down the path. "Where do you live?"

"Berview. Near caves, in forest. Time to leave. White men come. Kill us."

Nellie was aghast. "Surely not!"

"Were you at Loon Creek?" Charlie asked. He glanced at Nellie and Moonshine, giving a slight shake of his head.

All three men seemed to know that name. They began speaking at the same time. One shook his head and fell to his knees. Another one gestured to their spokesman, his eyes wide and his words agitated. "No, no!" The third man stopped the other two. "No danger here, now." He moved toward Nellie. "Woman safe." Moonshine barked once and stayed close to her, guarding her from anyone getting too close.

"You are safe with us," the sheriff said. "Are you certain you want to return to Bellevue? I can't keep you safe there." He gestured for all of them to walk back down the path. "Do you know anyone in Boise? There is a Joss House there. I can make sure you travel safely if you have friends or family. Maybe your tong will take you in." No one responded. "Think about it while we drive over the Pass." He whispered to Nell that a Joss House was a temple for the Chinese god, if there was such a thing.

In Ketchum, Charlie left Nellie and her dog at the boarding house. She wanted to ask him about Loon Creek, about these men, about a Joss House. Where would they be safe? He said, "I will talk to you later. Goldie can tell you." He knew what she was thinking. When they passed Last Chance Ranch, Nellie had thought to stop there and have the men camp out near Rosie and the boys, but that was not a good idea. She could see that Charlie had perhaps had the same idea, as he slowed the auto almost to a stop and then stepped on the gas again. He had glanced at Nellie and slightly shrugged his right shoulder, sighed, and said nothing.

Inside, the smell of fresh bread and a roast in the oven reminded Nellie that the picnic had been hours ago. She and Charlie had given the men their scraps. Two men from the Triumph Mine were already at the table, and Henry, the retired miner, soon joined them. Nellie stepped into the kitchen to tell Goldie she was home and could she help? Goldie shooed her out of the kitchen and soon carried in roast beef, potatoes, carrots, peas, bread, and gravy.

Nellie sat down in her accustomed place. When Goldie joined the group, Nellie asked her question. "What happened at Loon Creek?"

At first, no one said anything. They all kept eating. Finally, Goldie said, "Now where in the world did you hear about Loon Creek?" She set down her knife and fork and didn't wait for Nellie to respond. "Loon Creek is where nineteen Chinese men were massacred by the Sheepeater Indians. At least, that is what the authorities said. I have my doubts." Goldie picked up her utensils again and continued eating.

Henry added, "That was a long time ago, near forty years is my guess, or longer. No one ever got caught. The law said some renegade Indians did it, and they chased a few but didn't never catch a one. Forty years in this country is a long, long time."

One of the other miners chimed in. "Another massacre up on the Snake River near Oregon. Lots more murdered. No one charged with that either." He gave a short laugh. "Sure wouldn't want to be a Chinee in this mining country."

The telephone in the kitchen rang with two short blurts, the signal that the call was for the boarding house. "I'll get it, Goldie," Nellie said, and hurried out of the dining area. "Hello. Goldie's Rooming House." It was Charlie, reporting that he had dragooned Rosy into driving the three Chinese men to Boise in the morning.

"I just heard about Loon Creek and the Snake River massacres. How terrible! No wonder you wanted those men out of our area. How could the law let the murderers get away with such terrible crimes?"

75

"Lots of people around here thought Chinese were taking gold that wasn't theirs. Still do, I suspect. They were treated like animals, to the shame of most reputable souls. Both those events took place years ago, but I thought the Chinese men we picked up might be related to someone who died at Loon Creek. I asked them again, but they all shook their heads. They were too young to have been part of the group at Loon Creek. As far as I know, there were nineteen victims, but others could have escaped. Otherwise, I do not see how the Sheepeater Indians could have been blamed."

That was one of the longest speeches Nellie had ever heard Charlie give. "No one at our dining table thought the Indians did it either. They all knew of it, though." She paused a moment. "I need to take the train to Shoshone and go to Twin Falls to develop and print film. Do you have anything for me to do the next couple of days?"

"No. Go about your business. Can you return by the weekend? I would like to take you to dinner, just the two of us." His voice had dropped so low, Nellie wondered if someone were in his office with him.

"Yes, I'll be home. I would enjoy an evening with you—just the two of us. It seems we always have other people around us— Rosy, Chinese, Goldie." She smiled and felt as if she should say something more intimate. "See you then." She hung up, wondering if the telephone operator had been listening in.

*   *   *

Nellie stepped into Jacob Levine's photography studio. Both it and Twin Falls felt familiar to her after her absence to North Idaho and travels both ways. In her pack, she carried not only her camera, still needing to be repaired, but many pieces of film to be processed. True, she had been able to develop film she had taken in Bitterroot, Wallace and Mullen related to her and the sheriff's investigation there into bootleg activities and the mine explosion. Now, she had others she had taken on her own account, like the women at Mimi's bordello, around town, scenery when she, Rosy, Charlie and Moonie could stop on their return trip to Ketchum and Hailey. She had a couple from Vienna as well.

The studio seemed filled with people, and from what she quickly gathered, they weren't all happy people either.

"Mr. Levine, these prints are terrible! You must redo all of them." A stocky woman in hat and gloves and a skirt that hadn't yet made up its mind to be short or long but still constricting around her hefty-sized calves, fanned out five or six black and white photos. Nellie couldn't see their subject.

"Mrs. Stewart, these are photos I took at your daughter's wedding. I can't redo them." Jacob's face carried a slight sheen.

"But I am much too stout and far too short. My daughter's dress appears too small. Her bosoms look as if they're falling out of the dress!"

"The photos only show what was in front of the cameras," he said. He glanced over and saw Nellie. "I am sorry. I have other clients. I can make them softer with a diffuser but that will not change your height."

"Humph. Well, I never." She folded up her fan, stood from the chair, scowled at Nellie, and strode to the door. "Don't think I will ever hire you again." She opened the door, walked through, and slammed it.

"I've come at a bad time, it appears." Nellie sat on the chair which Mrs. Stewart had relinquished. It was still warm. She must have harangued for some time.

"Don't ever open a shop, Miss Burns. You'll regret it." Jacob pulled his chair tight to the desk. He pulled a plaid bandana from his pocket and wiped his face. "Warm in here, don't you think?" His receding hairline shone with the damp. She had grown fond of his face with its well-groomed beard and glasses. He was so conscientious. It was too bad a customer had maltreated him. She wondered if she would face the same kind of nasty customer in her studio.

Nellie nodded. "I would like to use your darkroom, Jacob, as we discussed on the telephone. Maybe I could take Mrs. Stewart's negatives and use a filter to soften the images while I am printing some film. Would that help?" She reached an arm across the desk.

"Miss Burns. Nellie. You are always so kind and generous." Jacob moved to cover her un-gloved hand. His was warm and squeezed just enough for her to feel it. "Would you marry me, Nellie? We have so much in common, and I have admired you from the moment you came into my studio months and months ago." His expression softened and his eyes held hers.

Nellie withdrew her hand. Was he serious? She couldn't tell. "Jacob, surely you have had a hard day! I admire you, too, but as one photographer to another." She smiled at him and hoped he didn't take offense at her light-hearted tone. "Besides, I am affianced already. Sheriff Azgo—Charlie—and I are getting married… in the fall." They hadn't decided on a date yet, but it seemed better to make a turn-down final.

"Oh." Jacob pulled his hand back as well. "Oh." A bit of a blush pinked his cheeks.

He had been serious.

"Maybe I should run some of my errands and come back a little later?" Nellie didn't want to embarrass Jacob. She liked the man and she still needed to use his dark room. "I am honored that you would ask me to marry you." She ducked her head as she could feel her own cheeks flushing. "You would make any woman a fine husband." She stood, not certain what to do.

Jacob cleared his throat. "Well, congratulations to you and to the sheriff, Nell. I do hope you will not give up your photography. You are a fine photographer and, if he does not mind, I hope we can continue to be colleagues. My darkroom is always open to you." His face turned a regular color, mostly pale, again. "Now, please let me see your camera so I can assess the damage."

"Of course, I will continue to photograph, Jacob. I haven't asked Charlie if he will mind. I have told him my plans." Maybe she should be more specific with Charlie, just in case he thought as Jacob did, that a woman must mind her husband.

Nellie opened her camera pack and then the camera. The bellows had been taped together by Walter Hope, the photographer in Bitterroot. He had used paper tape and the adhesion had lost its hold, so the paper was now crackling as she pulled out the bellows. Her shoulders sagged. The tear in the material had split even further. Clearly, this was not going to work. "Oh dear."

"There are better forms of tape now, Nell. This is a major tear, though." He fussed with the material and removed the paper tape. "I have a roll in my darkroom. Let me get it to see if I can patch the tear better. Otherwise, you may need a new camera, or at least a newer camera to you. Camera magazines always have ads for used machines." He stood, but hesitated. "You will have to tell me the story of how your camera was so damaged." His teeth gleamed in a large smile. "If I know you, it was something exciting."

"Yes, it was definitely exciting." Nellie was caught between holding back tears and returning Jacob's smile. He was such a nice man. But how could she afford a new, or even a used, camera?

In the darkroom, Nellie finished developing prints from the negatives she had brought to Twin Falls. She also did a proof sheet for Jacob of a wedding of a young couple on a spring day outside. She was particularly interested in what the bride wore. It was not a bouffant wedding dress, the current mode, but rather a flowered slender sheath fashion. Of course, all the photos were in black and white so she couldn't see the shades of the flowers, but she admired the lighting and use of shadow by Jacob. When she came out of the darkroom, Jacob greeted her at his front desk, seemingly none the worse for her turn-down.

"Nellie, thank you for your help. What is your project this time?"

"I am still working on photos from North Idaho and in the mine in Bitterroot but also a few back here—Galena Pass and Smiley Creek." Nell sat down. "Jacob, a terrible murder occurred along Smiley Creek among the Chinese. We have not found the perpetrator yet, but most assuredly it was white men or a white man. Do you still have a large population of Chinese here in Twin Falls?"

Jacob shook his head. "Only a few brave souls. Most were run out some years ago. It is a wonder anyone is following up on one murder. Your fiancé, I take it?"

Nellie felt herself blush again. "Yes. To him, a murder is a murder. He would follow it either way."

"I hope you were not present during the time." He lifted his hands as if to emphasize the point. "Was our acquaintance Sammy Ah Kee involved somehow?" Jacob had photographed Mrs. Ah Kee some time ago and helped Nellie recover a photo

Sammy had taken in the wrong assumption it was his father.

"No, although Sammy is the one who found the dead man in the water. He was extremely upset. I found him shortly after in a sal—café in Stanley." Nellie recounted her experience with Joe High Sing and later with Mrs. Ah Kee. A chill ran up her spine as she thought of the night and the moon. She still didn't know what happened to the body of Ah Kee, the herbal doctor.

"I am sorry you are involved in this, Nell. How does it happen that you seem to attract so many crimes?" The lines of Jacob's face deepened.

"As a crime photographer for Blaine County, that's why." Nellie laughed and stood. "At least now I am gainfully employed."

"Once you are married, you can go back to photography alone, I hope. A woman shouldn't be so involved with criminal detection. I suspect your future husband feels as I do."

Nellie didn't respond. She certainly hoped not. "I am on my way to see Gwynn this afternoon. He has not been well. Have you seen him?"

"Not since his fall. He is another one who takes too many chances. Riding a horse at his age did not bode well. Please give him my regards. And Nellie," Jacob said, paused and lowered his gaze, "please forgive my forwardness this morning."

"Nothing to forgive, Jacob. Any woman, I included, would be honored and complimented with the proposal you made." Nell quickly stepped to the door. "Goodbye for now."

*   *   *

Now that she could drive, Nell borrowed Franklin and Mabel's automobile at the rooming house in Twin Falls to motor out to Gwynn's ranch. She had called ahead from Ketchum and confirmed he would be there. His housekeeper Maria said he would enjoy the company, but that he had been cranky for some days now. Was she sure she wanted to visit?

It was time to tell Gwynn about her engagement. Charlie had said nothing about her trip to Twin to see her photographer colleague Jacob when she suspected most men would at least cast a suspicious eye. Or, at least that was her experience from watching her father and mother interact when Nellie was young, but old enough to notice. Her father, even after he left them to live apart, never ceased to ask questions and assume the worst about friends and, for all she knew of her mother, lovers. Her father would have been appalled at her mother's recent hint that the Negro professor at the college where she worked had been in touch. Nellie was happy her mother had found a male friend, even if people might consider it unusual.

At the house, Nell knocked on the front door. It seemed very quiet around the grounds, but of course, the sheep were off with Alphonso in the Basin and perhaps with other sheepherders in other places. She had no idea how many sheep Gwynn ran. Maria, Gwynn's soft-spoken and caring Spanish housekeeper, answered. "I am so happy you are here! Senor Campbell has been asking about you all morning. Please go up. He cannot get down the stairs with his wheelchair."

"Thank you, Maria." Nell would not have wanted to be Gwynn's caretaker. He was a fussy and cranky old man as often as he was a caring gentleman and knowledgeable rancher. He had taken care of her when she was in great need, so she could forgive him most faults. He disliked most of the people in Nellie's life, although he had softened considerably after last summer in the Stanley Basin.

And he loved his sheep dogs.

When Nellie entered Gwynn's large bed-sitting room, his face erupted in a huge grin, and she found herself grinning in return. He waved his arm from his sitting chair by the window. "You're definitely a sight for sore and beleaguered eyes, sweet Nellie! What took you so long?"

Up close, Nellie let him wrap his arm around her and kiss her cheek. "If I'd known how happy you would be to see me, I would have come much sooner!" She leaned over and kissed his cheek as well. His whiskers scratched her lips, but she didn't care. She could feel his affection for her. Maybe he hadn't saved her life up Fourth of July canyon, but he had given her help and good advice, as well as medical know-how. She rolled up her sleeve. "See? Hardly a whisper of a scar. You are the best doctor!" She rolled her sleeve down again and took his hand in a firm handshake. "I'm strong, too. No namby-pamby shake for me!"

Gwynn chuckled in his deep voice. "Sit down, Nellie. Tell me what is going on in your world. I know you were gone up north for weeks. Glad you are back in one piece. That is rough country up there—what with union wars and all. A little bird told me you went down the mine, too. Are you crazy?"

Who would have told him about her adventures? Maybe Rosy's sister. Goldie would not have been in contact, she was certain. "Have you seen the boys?" Nellie asked.

"Yes, I have. I convinced Rosy's sister Esther to bring them to see me when I couldn't get around. She hornswoggled Goldie into arranging a ride on the train and then Franklin to bring them out here." He smiled again, like the cat who swallowed a mouse. "I almost convinced her to stay with the boys and live here. But then Rosy came home with the two of you."

"They are at Last Chance Ranch this summer. You remember—"
Gwynn cut her off. "I remember. No need to bring that up." A
tear trembled in the corner of his eye.

Indeed not, Nellie thought, sorry she had mentioned it.
"Gwynn, we are involved in finding the murderer of a Chinese
man. What can you tell me about the history here and north?"

"Goldarn, them poor Orientals. Half the mining community was
after them all the time and the rest about half the time." His color
heightened, so Nell knew he felt better having something to talk
about other than the death of his daughter at Last Chance Ranch.
"I bet you've heard about the massacres in Idaho. Bloodthirsty
hooligans. I was just a young sprout then, but glad to be out here
in the country. A bunch of city fathers in Twin Falls insisted all
the Chinese leave town. Many did, but some stayed, saying they
hadn't been paid for laundry or food and they wouldn't leave until
they were. Some brave souls, in my opinion."

Nell wanted to ask Gwynn if he knew the Ah Kees, but she was
sure he would hate Ah Kee, the Celestial, for his opium practice.

"Ah Kee was one of 'em." Gwynn took a big breath and let it out.
"That damned Rosy told me what he did to try and save Lily. I
never knew his wife and son, but I'm sorry Ah Kee was murdered
the way he was."

What a change of heart, Nell thought. Rosy must have made a
good case for the herbalist and a sorry tale for what happened at
Last Chance Ranch. Either that, or Gwynn was getting soft in his
old age and pains. She reached for Gwynn's hand and held it in
both of her own. "Gwynn, I admire you for having the courage to
change your mind. Your life has not been easy." She squeezed, and
added, "And I have some good news for you, for once." She felt she
should gird her loins, whatever that meant. Charlie was one of the

people Gwynn had changed his mind about. Whether that would encompass the two of them getting together, Nell didn't know.

"Charlie and I are getting married. In the fall. We hope you can come to the wedding."

She waited for what? An explosion? Another grin?

"Ha, ha! I wondered when you'd tell me. I knew about that, too!" Gwynn patted her hand. "I think you could do better than a sheepherder-sheriff, but I won't complain. I did once and it cost me my daughter. I don't want to lose you." He paused and his mouth worked. "Congratulations, Nellie. You are like a daughter to me now." The tear finally ran down his cheek. "Look at me—waterworks half the time anymore."

Rosy's sister had certainly spread all the news. At least, she didn't tell Gwynn about the mudslide because Nellie had made Rosy promise not to say a word. She knew Charlie wouldn't.

"Would you like to see some of the prints I made at Jacob's studio?" She pulled her pack closer to get them out.

"I thought you and that Jacob man would get together. Then you'd live here in Twin and I'd see you all the time. But I'll not complain, Nellie." He raised his hand to stop anything she might say. "I... I... I... I wish you all happiness." Then he turned his attention to her photos.

They spent time over Nell's offerings. When she showed him the two photos—one from Galena Pass and one up Smiley Creek—Gwynn offered his comments. "Sounds like the miners are on the rampage again. A year or so ago, a Chinaman named Louie Joe, I think he was fairly young, died under suspicious circumstances and was buried in Hailey outside the gate." He shook his head. "The old prejudice just continues. You know Chinese still can't own land or be citizens, don't you?"

"Yes, Goldie told me that. The miners talked around the dinner table at the boarding house. No one seemed sad that the Chinese were mostly gone or couldn't be citizens. I'm glad I'm not Chinese. Mrs. Ah Kee and Sammy have difficult lives in Hailey. I thought they owned their house there along the river, but I guess they don't. I wonder who rents it to them."

"All the houses along River Street were burned out in 1920. A bunch of tunnels were found under the houses. Men smoked opium in those tunnels. There were even separate rooms." Gwynn glanced at Nellie. "Your friends probably furnished the opium to them. It wasn't strictly illegal in those days." He snorted. "Not like liquor in these days!"

Chapter 9

WHEN ROSY, CHARLIE, MOONIE AND Nell rode back from North Idaho in Rosy's automobile, she sat in back with her dog. In a way, she felt like a second-class citizen. Men in front. Women in back. It made sense, though, because Charlie drove and Rosy was really too big to sit in back. It was cramped space. Let it go. What she really wanted was to ride with Charlie without Rosy, so the two of them could talk. Nellie wanted to talk about their engagement. Did they really mean it? Were they in love with each other? Or was it a matter of convenience and not being able to name Nell as a deputy because she was a woman? She hated to think that, yet in a way Charlie was an extremely practical person. This might have been his way to have a deputy without naming Nell officially, which he was probably willing to do. He had broken one barrier just by being who he was and becoming sheriff. Another barrier might mean little to him. It would mean something to the people in Blaine County. They may have voted for him as a joke, but then found out he did the best job a sheriff had done in this county in many a year. Having a woman deputy, though, would have broken too many barriers. Women were supposed to be at home, cooking for their men and having children. That was one too many barriers for Nellie Burns.

So, Charlie and Nell didn't talk about being engaged and Rosy mostly slept. And when they arrived back in Hailey and Ketchum, they dropped Rosy off at Charlie's house in Hailey where the boys and Rosy's sister also lived, and then on to Ketchum to Mrs. Bock's boarding house. Goldie's house—their mutual home. Charlie stayed there for a while, until all the living arrangements could be sorted out.

That was last spring. As soon as summer arrived, Rosy and the boys moved to Last Chance Ranch and Charlie back to his own house in Hailey. Crime in Blaine County leaped in late spring and early summer and Charlie and Nell worked together—she taking photographs and he investigating and arresting. They worked together well—friendly, efficient, accomplished. Not the most deadly of crimes: public drunkenness (always), automobile wrecks caused by the previous crime, petty theft (mostly children), larceny and burglary (seldom as few people had anything to steal in Blaine county), embezzlement, barroom— oops, café—fights. A few calls to the local red light house to pick up surly clients who beat on a "soiled dove" or threatened to. That reminded Nellie of Bitterroot and Wallace. The police claimed the extra work there was why the cities charged fees for the "soda parlors."

When Nellie returned from Twin Falls, she arranged with Charlie to go to dinner in Hailey at the Hiawatha Hotel. She wore the same lavender dress she'd worn to the dance in Bitterroot when she'd felt so pretty and danced with both Charlie and Rosy. The sheriff didn't arrive in the police automobile, but instead drove an auto he borrowed from someone in Hailey. He wore his Basque vest and polished cowboy boots, not his working boots. His hair was slicked back, ebony black but with some gray around his temples. What a handsome man he was. Few people knew they were engaged, but Goldie and Rosy knew. Even Moonshine seemed to suspect something. He nosed Charlie along his leg and rubbed his head on Charlie's hand. Nell fluttered around, feeling nervous and delighted at the same time. She hoped he didn't intend to break off their engagement. He had hardly referred to it since Nell said yes to his proposal in the Callahan Hotel. He knew what he was getting, she thought. Even down to her underwear in a bathtub. Nell still blushed to think he had undressed her and warmed her in the tub at the hotel. Of course, he saved her life. But she had a turn in saving his. They had never talked about that either. The thought of what she'd done came to her fairly frequently, often at night. Maybe she felt guilty. Not much, though.

At the door, when Nellie greeted Charlie, he picked her up by her waist and swung her around. "I liked dancing with you, Nell. Wish we could do it again." He held Nell close. No, he wasn't going to break off their engagement.

Nell called out to Goldie: "We're on our way, Goldie. We may be late." She smiled up at Charlie. He was more than a head taller than she was, and in his boots, maybe more than that. Her slippers had small heels that made her feel tall, even though she wasn't. Nell's hair was dark brown, not black, and her skin fairer than his. Still, Nell thought they made a handsome couple, all dressed up with somewhere to go. Goldie came out to the hall. She smiled, a somewhat rare occurrence.

"Now ain't you two fancy." She hugged herself. "Young and in love, I can see. If I weren't so steeped in age, I'd feel jealous. Instead, I'm happy for you." Then, she turned and headed back to her kitchen, her home within the house, and her hideaway.

"Come along, Moonshine. They don't need you tonight." And he followed, looking back at Nellie. He looked as if he were smiling, too. "I'll leave a light on for you, but don't hurry back," Goldie called.

Nellie felt her face begin to blush, so she pulled a shawl from the front closet and swirled it around her. "I'm ready, my handsome cavalier." Now what made her say that?

"Ah, my lovely princess. Let's climb into our steed and head down the road." Charlie sounded more light-hearted than she had ever heard him.

In the auto, Charlie turned to Nellie as he steered to Hailey. "You wore that dress at the dance in Bitterroot, didn't you?" Nellie nodded. "I was proud to be your escort. Maybe that was when I knew I wanted you in my life—then and always."

Nellie didn't know what to say. No one had ever spoken such words to her, and she felt her tongue stick in her mouth. She scooted closer to Charlie and felt his strong leg next to hers, except the gear shift stuck up between them. "Thank you," was all she could mumble.

"Although, you were also fetching when you were covered in mud and your eyes looked haunted and your hand was stuck in my belt." Charlie laughed and put his arm around her. "I had no idea you were so strong. Although I was weak from working in that rock burst. Thank you for all you did."

At the restaurant, Charlie led Nellie to a table in shadows near the back, lit only by a small candle. "This was as fancy as I could find, Nellie. I hope it suits you. We need to talk, something we have had no time for since our trip home with our chaperone, Rosy." He seated Nellie and placed her wrap on the back of her chair. When he sat down, Nellie noticed he faced the rest of the room and the front door, just like a cowboy in one of those silent films. "I already ordered for both of us, a habit I promise I will not get into, but I did not want a waiter barging in and out while we are talking." His Basque accent seemed stronger than usual, Nellie thought. Maybe he was as nervous as she was.

Nellie was taken a little aback. Indeed, she preferred to order for herself. She liked doing everything for herself. She kept her lips closed and nodded at Charlie, waiting. He had something in mind, she was sure.

A waiter did bring a dark bottle, something that surely held alcohol, and two glasses. Good thing Charlie was the sheriff, she thought. Arresting himself might be hard to do. He poured a liquid that gleamed deep red in the candlelight on the table. Oh my, this is romantic, Nellie thought. She held up her glass and Charlie clinked his softly against hers. They each took a sip. The last time Nellie had tasted wine this delicious was in Chicago. She'd gotten used to the sheepherder wine the previous summer with Alphonso, and whatever Rosy had brought to the Craters of the Moon. None of them had so much as a sip of wine in North Idaho. They had been searching for bootleggers, after all. This was in a different class entirely.

When Nellie looked down, she saw a small box sitting in front of her. A velvet box. She had not seen Charlie bring it out, but he must have done. For me? she pantomimed. Charlie nodded. She opened it, her hands shaking ever so slightly. At twenty-six, she had never imagined this would happen to her. Inside the dark velvet, a ring shone: two diamonds, one larger than the other, and a green stone offset between them. Smaller diamonds circled the arrangement. Nellie held her breath. "Oh, Charlie! This is beautiful!" She picked up the ring and held it in the palm of her hand. "You shouldn't have!" How many women had said the same thing? Not many, she acknowledged to herself. But she knew the county paid Charlie only a middling salary and travel expenses, surely not enough to buy such an expensive piece of jewelry.

"No?" Charlie smiled. He took the ring and held her left hand, placing the ring on her fourth finger. "I am sorry this took so long to give to you. I wired the jeweler in Twin Falls when we were in Bitterroot and told him what I wanted. The emerald is for your eyes, although they look smoky gray at this moment. The diamonds are for your heart. This will have to do for our wedding, too."

"Have to do?" Nellie held Charlie's hand. "I have never seen such an unusual and beautiful ring. It will not leave my finger." She wanted another one of those soul kisses he had given her in Bitterroot, but leaning across the table didn't seem quite appropriate, especially since several people had entered the restaurant and appeared quite interested in them. As did the waiter. He hovered at a respectful distance, but definitely hovered. "Just don't let me get my hand stuck in your belt again." They both laughed. The waiter brought their dinners—lamb shanks with mashed potatoes and asparagus. The waiter frowned at Nellie. She giggled quietly. He must have thought she said something untoward.

Neither one said anything for the space of several minutes as they began to eat. Charlie poured Nellie and then himself more red wine. Nellie worried someone might report them to the revenuers. It would be a scandal—sheriff and police photographer drinking alcohol as scofflaws in a restaurant in Hailey. Except Charlie was the one who usually reported federal crimes to the authorities. Stop it, Nellie, she told herself. Just be quiet and relax. This is a special occasion.

"When?"

Charlie's voice startled Nellie. "When what?"

He laughed. "What do you think? Get married." His grin was as big as the Cheshire Cat's in Alice in Wonderland. Nellie thought hers must be almost as wide.

Nellie held out her left hand, admiring the ring. "This fall? At Last Chance Ranch? After all, that is where we met."

Chapter 10

SAMMY LEARNED FROM MISS BURNS about the three Chinese men rescued from the white men. The miner Rosy took them and helped them into the Chinese temple—the Joss House—in Boise. One man, somewhat older, spoke some English. Miss Burns said she could never understand their names, but she would ask Rosy when he returned.

In times past, Sammy's mother told him, many Chinese lived in Idaho and many stayed in Hailey and Bellevue. It was against the law for Chinese to work in mines or claim their own finds. Instead, they operated laundries and cafés. All except his father who used herbs and opium to save Chinese lives, until he was murdered at Last Chance Ranch.

Miss Burns wanted Sammy to show her where Hung Lui was buried so Sheriff Azgo could confirm the murder and seek the criminal who did it. No other sheriff has ever looked for killers of Chinese. White men dressed as Indians killed Chinamen, so the Indians would be blamed. White men killed Chinese even without dressing as Indians.

Sam would find who killed Hung Lui. That was his job to do.

Mother did not like Hung Lui, but it would have been difficult for her to cut his throat. She could have hired it done. Would she have talked to a white man? Would he have paid her any mind?

Silver dollars spoke loudly. His mother placed her dollars in a wooden box that read Tea in Chinese. Sammy had looked into that box and it was empty.

Mr. Rosy was a miner. Maybe he would tell Sammy who might have used Chinese workers to find gold. Sam dreamed of showers of gold coins in Vienna, the ghost town, where the Chinese men were found and the sheriff and Miss Burns released them. If they did hide gold, the white men would return. Sammy would go there and search. How to do that? No one would take him except Miss Burns. Sammy cannot put her in danger. He would get a gun to keep her safe.

Chapter 11

NELL KNEW CHARLIE WOULD DISAPPROVE of her taking Sammy Ah Kee to Vienna, but he was called to Stanley to meet with a forest ranger who needed help with what sounded like an incipient range war. Gwynn Campbell had asked him to go, too, in his place to represent him—an ironic turnaround from the days Gwynn had distrusted Charlie. Gwynn said Charlie knew sheep and wouldn't be steamrolled by the cattle men.

Sammy tried to borrow the cobbler's automobile, but the cobbler said no. Sammy telephoned Nell on the shoe shop telephone and asked if she would take him to Vienna. She said she would if he would show her where Hung Lui was buried so she could take a photograph. He hemmed and hawed and finally said he would do so.

The Chinese man met Nell in Ketchum by hitching a ride. Nell picked him up at the butcher shop. Sammy said no Moonshine, so Nell dropped her dog off with Goldie, who frowned when told their destination. "I hope you know what you're doing."

They motored over Galena Pass in Henry's car, borrowed by Nell again. She could have asked Rosy to come along, but she hesitated to do so. He would also object. They left early in the morning because it would take several hours to get there.

Worried about meeting up with the man that she and Charlie

had met, Nell slowed down and stopped several curves before the ghost town. "We walk from here," she said. Sammy did not argue as Nell pulled the auto off to the side of the road and stopped it in the shade of several trees. It wasn't hidden, but anyone would have a difficult time seeing it if they hurried on the road to Vienna. Nell lifted her pack from the boot and strapped it on her shoulders, ignoring Sammy's offer to carry it.

They proceeded slowly up the road until Nell could see whether anyone was in sight in the abandoned buildings. She heard no sounds, saw no one and no autos. She did remember that she and Charlie had seen no one either and that Bubba's auto was hidden in a shed. She motioned to Sammy to move behind one building, and she stepped as softly as she could to another. They waited a while and still heard nothing and saw no one. Finally, Nell moved out in the open. Sammy joined her. Nell, using a low voice, said, "The mill building up there is where we found the Chinese men." She pointed and then turned and gestured toward another two-story building. "We think that was the boarding house. A former saloon is along that path." Another turn.

Sammy hurried toward the mill. When Nellie caught up, she found him inside and checking the walls and floor, as well as any possible cubbyholes. He had told Nell he thought he could find any gold the men had panned. Nell glanced around but thought the miners would have taken anything the Chinese had found before they locked them up. Still, the Chinese were smart and might not have disgorged everything they found, possibly risking being beaten or killed for withholding gold.

Nellie heard an automobile and hurried to the door to close it. She peeked to see if she knew the auto and saw that it was coming downhill rather than up. The old mine entrance was up the road so whoever it was had been at the closed up-entrance. Why? The mine had not been operated for years—forty or more. The auto continued its way through the ghost town. Although not certain, Nellie thought she recognized the driver as one of the three men she'd seen on her earlier trip into Smiley Creek. It wasn't Bubba, but it might have been the man called Hank.

Sammy huddled behind Nell. "Do you recognize man?" He whispered the words.

"Maybe." When the auto stopped at the very end of the tumbling-down structures, she closed the door completely, hoping whoever was in the automobile would not get out and wander around. She had no weapon, and the men might shoot Sammy. It seemed that was what happened whenever Celestials labored in a mining camp. She heard conversation, but the men were too far away for her to understand what was being said. Soon, the motor started up again and Nellie opened the door a crack to see the auto disappear down the roadway. She kept her fingers crossed that they would not see her automobile in the trees.

After a lengthy wait, Nellie opened the door to the mill. "Are you still looking for gold?" She stepped outside. "I think we should walk up the road to the mine entrance and see what might be going on there."

"I stay here and search more. You go ahead." Sammy began poking around where the ground met the walls of the building. "I know there are gold coins in here."

"Sammy, where would the men get gold coins? They were panning for gold. If there is anything, it will be gold dust or maybe even nuggets. Not gold coins." Nellie could swear Sam blushed.

"No, no. I meant gold powder." He dropped to his hands and knees and crawled around the inside of the space. It was dark in the mill, although sunlight came in through the door. He patted the ground, moved a yard, and patted again.

"All right. I will walk up the road. I'll shout if I see anything worth exploring." The way climbed in a steep path hardly wide enough for an auto. Within minutes, Nellie could no longer see the collapsed town when she looked behind. Ahead, there appeared to be a cave in the mountain wall, a cave that was the defunct Vienna mine. There were boards. In front of the boards leaned what looked like a metal cage closing off the entrance to the workings. It was clear to Nell that the men were hiding something or guarding someone. She wished Sammy were with her, or someone. She didn't want to explore on her own. That was always how she got into trouble.

Nell decided to photograph the cage. Something was wrong here and she wanted proof. She lowered her pack and pulled out her camera and tripod. Then she heard voices behind her. One was Sammy's, talking loudly, almost shouting. Nell turned to face her friend and whoever was behind him, pushing. Sam walked in tiny steps and stumbled onto his face. Nell rushed to help him up but the man—it was Bubba—shoved her away.

"You're that snoop who let our workers out, you—"

"And you're the monster who kept those men trapped with no water or food." She hoped he still didn't have the revolver he had dropped when Charlie challenged him. "What are you doing with this man? He is not one of your minions." Nell tried to keep her voice as steady as she could, even though inside she did not feel steady at all. "Untie him. No one can walk that way." She retreated to protect her camera equipment.

"Why do you care? He's a Chink, an alien. It's against the law for him to attack me. I'm holding him until the law comes to arrest him." He held up a revolver. "I found this on him."

Nell glanced at Sam, who lowered his head. "We carried a gun to protect against bears," she said. "That one is mine. Please give it to me." She held out her hand, but Bubba slid the weapon into his ample waist band.

"Nah, it's mine now. Where's your lawman friend?" Bubba looked around the area by the mine adit. "Hiding? He ain't so brave here, is he?" He pushed Sam forward again, passing Nell as if she weren't there.

"Stop! Let him go. I'll see that you are punished for this and for kidnapping those Chinese men we released."

"You and who else? Be careful, or I'll put you in that cage, too. Then we'll see who punishes who. You're a hussy, miss, ain't you? Talkin' pretty big for such a small thing. Maybe we'll see who can boss me." He leered at her. He shoved Sammy again, this time down in the dirt, and he grabbed Nellie by her arm. With his other arm, he swung her toward him and hugged her close. "You smell good." He rubbed his whiskery face against hers while she struggled to free herself. Her hand squeezed against the revolver. She pulled it out and jerked backward as hard as she could. She managed to stay on her feet, and Bubba lost his balance and landed on his butt. By then, Sammy had recovered and flung himself on Bubba's head, and, with a rock in his hand, hit Bubba's head, hard.

"Stop, Sammy! Move away. I have the gun. Take off your ropes, so you can stand up."

Bubba moaned. Blood flowed down the side of his head from his left ear, which was torn. "He tried to kill me. He'll pay for this!" Bubba tried to get up.

"Stay there, Mister Bubba. I have the gun now." She held it pointed at the man. "Give Sammy the key to that cage. I suspect you have more Chinese in there." She shifted the gun to the side and pulled the trigger. A huge blast roared and dirt and rocks scattered every which way in the dusty ground surrounding the mine adit and cage. Her arm ricocheted back, but she hung on to the weapon. Bubba at last looked scared and tossed a ring of keys to Sammy.

"Tie him up, Sammy. I want to take a photograph. Then we'll use the keys on that cage." Nellie waited until Bubba was secure, and then she propped her camera on the tripod, covered herself with the black cloth and focused her camera. Jacob had repaired it as much as he could, but even as she readied to take the photo, she knew she would have to get a new camera. The black cloth came off, she inserted the film carrier, pulled out the black slide and released the shutter. Now she had memorialized the place. She nodded to Sammy.

Bubba had scooted himself around so he could see what Sam was doing. She could see he worked at the rope that tied his hands behind his back. Sam tried several keys and finally found one that worked. The door of the cage swung open. Behind it, there was nothing but black, presumably a tunnel leading into the mountain that loomed up behind, covered with grasses and small trees. Sam began to enter. He called into the darkness, "Hey. Anybody there?"

"Don't go in, Sammy. We don't know what is in there. It could be a trap." Nell looked at Bubba. "Get Mister Bubba on his feet and send him in. If anyone or thing is waiting to pounce, they can pounce on him."

Bubba had seemed calm when Sammy was trying out the various keys. Nell wondered why he hadn't been at least agitated if there were more men held in the cage or behind it. She had laid down the revolver while taking the photograph, but she picked it up again. Her Chinese friend approached Bubba and grabbed his arm to pull him up. Bubba jerked it away.

"Don't touch me, you filthy Chink."

Sam kicked him in the belly and pulled again at the prone man's arm. "Up, up, up."

Nellie winced, but she wasn't going to say anything. Bubba had certainly mistreated Sam Ah Kee and deserved whatever Sammy handed out. Still, she joined the other two and pulled on Bubba's second arm. Between them, they got the heavy man to his feet. Now, Sammy pushed him toward the gate. At the opening, Sammy shoved the man, forcing him through the gate and past the cage toward the wood barrier. Bubba stumbled and fell forward. His hands were tied so he could not save himself and he fell on his hurt ear. He howled.

"Let's go in, Sammy, but just as far as Bubba is in." Nell stepped as slowly as Sammy did as they passed the entrance and stood beside their captive. He moaned but didn't try to stand up again.

Sammy glanced around and dropped to his knees. "What in here?" He shouted at Bubba. "Men? Gold?" Sam crawled over to the inner wall, stood up, and kicked at what looked like a sluice box. On the second kick, it fell apart and revealed several dark bags, tied at the top, with leather straps. "Aha!"

Bubba moaned again. Nell joined Sammy at the box. She leaned over and lifted one of the bags. It was heavier than it looked. "Sammy, we may have found your gold coins."

Again on his knees, Sammy pulled at one of the bags and opened the leather strap. He peered in. He opened the top even further and jabbed his hand in, bringing out a shower of gold powder, laced with small nuggets. He glanced over at Bubba and looked up at Nellie. "This is gold from Chinese-not-Chinese—men in Smiley Creek that Hung Lui and I saw. The men you and sheriff saved." He hugged himself. "I keep some and give rest to them."

"What about Hung Lui? Does he have any family here?" Nell kept an eye on Bubba and on the gate. The man Bubba had been with in the automobile might come back. She and Sammy needed to leave as soon as possible.

Sammy's face turned down. "Hung Lui." He turned to Bubba and moved to kick him again.

"Sammy, no more kicking. We don't know if Bubba was the one who killed your friend."

"You kill Hung Lui?" Sammy shouted into Bubba's face. He turned to Nellie. "You go get motorcar and drive up here. I wait." He held his hand out. "Give me gun."

Against her better judgment, Nellie decided to do as Sammy asked, even though it sounded more like an order. She hurried down the road, tripping some over rocks and grass bunches, until she arrived at her auto. She drove back to the Vienna mine and backed up to the entrance. When she entered, Sammy still waited by Bubba, but she could see the prone man's face had another smudge and his shirt was untucked. Sammy had taken more revenge. She would deal with that problem later. "If you want this gold, Sammy, you must load it yourself. It is too heavy for me." She walked up to Bubba. "I will help you sit up and then we will leave you here. We'll tell the sheriff, and he can come and get you if he is so moved. Don't count on it, though." She knew Charlie would not leave a man trapped in the mine. He would come and charge Bubba with something—kidnapping, stealing, assault and battery.

"You can't leave me here. Please, missy. I'm sorry I called you a hussy. Don't leave me alone up here." Bubba was near to tears. "Them ghosts'll come and kill me." He tried to get up on his own but could not. "Take the gold. Just don't leave me."

Chapter 12

NELLIE DROVE THE AUTO DOWN the road from the Vienna Mine. Sammy had insisted he should drive, but she ignored him. This was Henry's auto, and she was responsible. Actions by the Chinese man had disturbed her, not least his mistreatment of Bubba, who probably deserved it. No, Sammy's reaction to the gold seemed to change his personality completely. From a quiet, kind man, he turned into an abusive gold seeker and petty tyrant. She wondered if he really would turn over the gold to the sheriff, where it belonged until its true owner could be determined, although she wouldn't object to Sammy receiving a reward of some sort. She wanted nothing to do with it. Don't be so virtuous, she told herself. She needed a new camera.

As they reached the rickety bridge over Smiley Creek, another automobile plugged the road, heading in their direction. Nell slowed and pulled as much as she could to the side to let the auto pass. The road was narrow, and she wasn't certain it could do so. As it neared her, she saw it was the sheriff, Charlie.

He stopped right alongside her. "I thought you were settling a range war," she said through her opened window. She tried not to show her pleased surprise but failed because she couldn't help smiling at him.

"And I thought you were not going exploring on your own

again." Charlie's face didn't exactly smile, but his eyes did.

"I didn't. Here is Sammy Ah Kee." Nell gestured to Sammy and turned toward him. He had slumped way down in his seat so that the sheriff, or anyone else in the automobile, couldn't see him. "Sammy, sit up. It's the sheriff, not Bubba's companion."

"Was Bubba up there?" The light went out of the sheriff's black eyes and his demeanor turned somber again.

"Yes." Nell shrugged her shoulders. "It's a long story, but the upshot is that we left him locked inside the mine adit and we took several bags of gold dust." She could sense Sammy's distress at revealing the presence of gold. "Sammy discovered the gold. Without him there, I would never have found it. He should get a reward." The Chinese man relaxed somewhat, and Nell did not add that without Sam, she wouldn't even have been there. And without him, Bubba might have seriously harmed her. She reached her hand out to Charlie. "Do you want to take the gold now? I would feel better if it were in your control." She saw Sammy move his arm in a negative gesture, a quick back and forth, but she pretended not to see it.

"Is Bubba alone?" The sheriff left Nell's arm hanging.

"He is at the moment. Earlier, he either drove or accompanied another man in an auto coming down from the mine. The entrance has a cage on it, so we thought there might be more Chinese men hidden in the mine." Nell glanced at Sammy. He shook his head, frowning in an almost exaggerated fright face. She whispered, "What is wrong with you, Sammy?" Nell grimaced back.

"I've been afraid the other man would come back. The auto was old, maybe Model T old, dusty and shabby. It even had a crank on the front. It was not the one Bubba drove out of the ghost town when we visited." Even as she spoke, she saw dust rising and heard the rumble and clank of an automobile coming out of the woods behind Charlie. "That might be him, now."

Charlie looked in his side mirror. "You and Sam stay here. I will go see who and what this person is and wants."

"His name might be Hank," Nell said. She brought her arm back into the auto and pointed with her other arm to the passenger well. "Sammy," she whispered, "crouch down again. We don't want him to see you."

Nell couldn't be certain if it was the same automobile as she and Sammy had seen earlier but probably not. She didn't see a crank in the front. The sheriff took his time. He conducted a long conversation with the driver. After a while, the man opened the door and stepped out. He gestured toward the creek and the two of them walked over to the edge. Nell did not recognize the man, although his slick-backed hair seemed familiar. Of course, many men wore their hair that way. It was not Hank. Still, she had not seen the third man when she and Sammy hid along the trail when they sought the gold panning site earlier.

Both men laughed and shook hands. Charlie came back and climbed into his motor car and moved several lengths ahead, so the other auto could get by Nell. The man had donned a slouchy hat, and although she scrutinized the man as he passed, she couldn't see his features. He waved and hardly glanced at her. Then Charlie backed up to rest his auto beside her again.

"Fisherman," he said. "I will take the gold and meet you back in Ketchum after I go rescue Bubba. I suspect he will be surprised to see me."

"How do we know you won't steal the gold," Sammy called across Nellie.

Charlie answered. "You do not, except Miss Burns here would roast me alive."

At last Sammy lost his grim expression. He turned to Nell. "True?"

"True," Nell said.

*　*　*

"All right, Sammy. It is time for you to fulfill your half of the bargain." Nell glanced at Sammy, as she put the auto into gear. "Where is Hung Lui buried?" She would tell Charlie about the reason she had driven her Chinese friend back to the Vienna mine later. A lie of omission, she thought. She had said it was a long story, though.

After Charlie's auto disappeared around a bend in the road, Nell pulled over into her previous spot. "Are we close here?"

Sammy looked anywhere but at Nell. His head tilted from right to left and back again. He turned and faced her. "You do not want to see Hung Lui," he said.

"But I do. I can photograph where he is buried and the sheriff can dig him up. He needs a body to prove he was murdered."

The man sat in silence. He began to mouth words several times, but each time shook his head to himself. Finally, the words came out. "He is not buried. I promise him I send his bones back to China. He is in open air."

"What do you mean, you promised. You said he was dead when you found him." Nell could hardly keep herself from shrinking back from Sammy. Had Joe High Sing been right, and it was Sammy who killed his friend?

"We vowed when we crossed border into *Amelica*." Sammy

hung his head. "When I found him, I promised again to his spirit. I could not do otherwise. No one finds him where he is." He talked into his chest. "And if they do, Hung Lui's ghost will hide him." This time, Sammy looked up and into Nell's eyes. "Please. We do not disturb him."

"Sammy, we need proof that he is dead and that you did not kill him." She waited for a response. None came. "A photograph will at least confirm he is dead. It will not prove you innocent of Joe's charge against you. Anyone who knows you also knows you would not kill a man." She was not so sure of this anymore.

"If I take you, and you photograph Hung Lui, his ghost will wander forever. It will not let you rest or let me rest. It is the wrong thing to do." His voice dropped lower and lower.

"Then why did your mother force me to photograph your father. No one said anything about ghosts, then." Nellie rubbed her arm, the one Bubba had grabbed and twisted. She wanted to go home.

"I begged her not to do so. His ghost has been haunting her ever since. Now that he has been moved, we can send his bones back to China." He waved in the air toward his country. "Soon."

"A deal is a deal, Sammy Ah Kee. You cannot back out on it now." Nellie wasn't sure she wanted to press the issue, but she knew she needed the photo, and if she didn't get it now, when would she?

Her Chinese friend began walking. He took a barely visible side path off the main trail along the river. It led to thick shrubbery, and they had to force their way through it. Then there were rocks and dirt and more rocks. The path disappeared, what she could see of it anyway. Sammy knew where he was going. Through more shrubs and small trees. Taller trees shaded them as they pushed and stumbled along. Sammy abruptly stopped. "There." He pointed toward a scooped-out section of rock and dirt. On it lay a body, its clothes in tatters, its face mostly devoured, and the whole corpse swollen to be almost unidentifiable except as a human. The limbs appeared to have been attacked by birds or vultures or even a coyote, one leg bare to the bones, maggots crawling on and around the flesh that was left.

Nellie turned her head, the smell too much to bear. She stepped backwards. This was her own fault. Sammy had tried to tell her. She turned her back to the corpse, wishing she had not seen it, knowing it would be in her dreams for nights to come, maybe forever. Her previous experience taking photographs of embalmed dead people for loving families and before funerals didn't compare to this sight in any way. Nell loosened her pack, brought out her camera and tripod.

"I need to take a photograph, Sammy. Help me." Her plea brought Sammy around. He picked up the tripod and set it so the camera would look at the face and neck, the pertinent parts of the body. Nellie fastened the camera, covered herself with the black cloth, and tried to focus the lens on the neck, which no longer showed any blood, if it ever did after being in the water. Maggots swarmed. Nausea flooded her. She dropped the cloth and turned aside to throw up, even though there was little in her stomach. The acid burned the back of her throat.

"Do you want me to take the picture?" Sammy hovered. He placed his hand on her back and patted. "It won't be long now before I can scrape the bones and send them to China."

The words made Nellie gag again. Nothing this time. "I'll do it." Her voice rasped. She picked up the cloth, this time focused. Again, she dropped the cloth, pulled out the film carrier, inserted it and took the photo. "I can't do anymore. Let's go." As quickly as she could, Nell repacked the tripod and camera into her pack, hefted it to her shoulder and began to walk back through the shrubs.

"I will lead, Miss Burns. Follow me."

Nellie stumbled and nearly fell twice but caught herself. The air did clear, and she filled her lungs with the scent of evergreens and eventually the river water. Back at the auto, she handed the key to Sammy. "You drive."

* * *

The gruesome odor and image stayed with Nellie. She wondered if her clothes would carry the smell forever, or if her nose would ever be rid of it. She thought of the dead body in the ice cave. The cold there had dissipated any smell. The same with the other caves. Even the makeshift morgue at the butcher's shop had no smell that she could remember.

Agitation filled Nell with the urge to get out and walk. Finally, she could feel her muscles begin to calm. She had smelled nothing over the empty hole in the woods where Sammy's father had been buried. She watched out the window of her auto, trying to replace the horrid image of maggots and insects with green evergreens and bright spring green of aspens, always slow to leaf out in this north country.

Getting back to Ketchum and Hailey took as long as driving the other way. Nell broached the subject of Ah Kee to Sammy. "What happened to your father's... body?" Sammy had said it was Chinese business and none of hers.

"My honored mother moved him." Neither said anything more.

When they approached Last Chance Ranch, Nellie leaned toward Sammy. "Go in there. I would like to visit Rosy and the boys." She couldn't tell Rosy where they had been, but maybe the smell of lavender planted all around the cabin, and the company would help remove the grisly scene from her mind's eye. "You remember Rosy, don't you? Have you met the boys?"

Sammy shook his head, but he seemed relieved to have a distraction, too.

The long driveway led to the house, now improved with another wing. Rosy must have built that section. The boys played tag or a game—Matt taller and darker and Campbell shorter and lighter. They dashed up to the automobile as its occupants stepped out. "Nellie! Nellie!" She had given them permission to use her first name, much to Goldie's annoyance.

"Matt, Campbell. This is Sammy Ah Kee. Sammy, these are Rosy's boys." She hesitated a moment. "Matt is the older and Campbell the younger."

Sammy bowed his head, then looked up and smiled, something Nell had not seen in days and maybe months. His teeth did not look in good shape. He had worn his Oriental hat the whole day, but now took it off.

Matt's and Campbell's eyes widened. They must have realized that he was Chinese.

Rosy stepped off the porch, a long stick in his hand. "Hiya Nellie. I been whittlin' on a walkin' stick for you." He held it out. "It's oak and pretty strong. Maybe you can use it." He winked. "You might could keep discipline with it. Try it on for size." He turned to Sammy and put out his hand. They shook, but each dropped his hand quickly.

Nellie took what was really a short pole. She held it near the top where Rosy had carved a sitting dog—Moonshine. "Rosy, it's wonderful. Look at Moonshine!" She turned to look back at the auto. "Unfortunately, Moonie is not with us today. We've been visiting the Vienna Mine ghost town."

"Have a seat on the porch, you two. I'll mix up some lemonade. Boys, get a coupla chairs out for our company." He waved his hand. "Don't get much company up here. Good for the boys to have room to play, though."

The scent of the lavender, just beginning to bloom, was heavenly to Nell's nose. Bees buzzed, dozens of them. She breathed in deep, glanced at Sammy, and followed the boys up onto the porch. "The lavender is just right," she said. She wondered if the sheriff had already picked up Bubba and driven back to Hailey. He could have done so while they tramped through the woods to find Hung Lui. She closed her eyes, willing herself to fill her head with the aroma of lavender. The scent reminded her of another time at Last Chance Ranch when she had found small bags of lavender and—.

"We built a fort, Nellie. And Mr. Awkee. Want to see it?" Campbell jumped up and down.

"Yes! As soon as we have some of your father's lemonade." Nell's mouth was dry as a white, brittle bone. No! No more images!

"We found something else, too. Wait 'til you see it," Matt said. His eyes twinkled.

After they finished their refreshments, the boys led Nellie to the woods below the cabin, where once Nell and the sheriff had found a body. They walked even farther until Matt stopped. "There." He pointed toward a small mound.

At first, Nell couldn't understand what the boy wanted her to see. She walked closer and then saw a weathered board. On it was the word "Unknown."

"Who is it?" she whispered.

"No one knows," Campbell said. "We asked at the store up the road. And it does say 'Unknown.'"

Nellie realized she might know who "Unknown" was but declined to say. She had her own ghosts from her first adventures at Last Chance Ranch. Too many ghosts.

Chapter 13

WHEN NELL DREW THE PHOTOGRAPH of Hung Lui out of the fixer in her makeshift darkroom in Goldie's rooming house, she didn't feel the same nausea as in the forest. Maybe because the scene was in black and white, and truly, it was almost impossible to decipher what was in the photo. She wanted to deliver it to the sheriff—Charlie—as soon as she could. She had not heard from him since her return to Ketchum, but that wasn't unusual. He would have processed Bubba and delivered him to the jail in Hailey.

A tap on the door interrupted her musings. "What is it?"

Goldie responded. "You have a visitor. Another one of them Chinese. Not Sammy. Shall I tell him you are too busy or not here?"

"Hmm. I'll be out in five minutes. Don't scare him away." It must be Joe High Sing. She knew of no other Chinese unless it was Mrs. Ah Kee, but Goldie would have said so.

In the salon, Joe High Sing did wait, seated with his hat on his knees. When Nellie entered the room, her photography studio, he stood up and bowed slightly. "Good morning, Joe." She reached out her hand, but Joe didn't take it.

"My leg better. Thank you for helping me." His apology sounded rehearsed. "Sam Ah Kee said you needed names from me."

"You've seen Sammy? Does that mean you don't blame him

115

anymore for Hung Lui's death?" That would be a relief, both for her and Sammy.

Joe's eyes opened and closed. The expression on his face reminded Nell of Charlie's—stony. "Sam carry Hung Lui. His throat cut."

"He must have told you what he was doing—placing Hung Lui in the open air so he could send the man's bones back to... to China." She didn't know how to pronounce the name Sammy had given her, both for Hung Lui and for his father.

Joe waved his hand, as if swatting away a fly. "You want names?"

"Yes, please. Let me get paper to write them down." Nellie decided she was not going to argue with Joe. She wanted his information to give to Charlie, so he, Rosy, or she could follow up in their investigation. She maintained a small desk in one corner of the room. She found paper and a pencil and sat down near Joe. "These are the men who panned for gold in Smiley Creek?" The man nodded. "Can you spell them for me?"

"Hung Lui, cannot spell." He said three more names and pronounced them quite slowly, again saying he could not spell. "All Chinese-not-Chinese." He patted the back of his neck where his braid hung down. "White men hide in forest. When they come out, I wade to shore and run. Bad men." Joe shook his head. "Bad men."

"One of those bad men murdered Hung Lui," Nellie said. "If Sammy had returned earlier, he would have been murdered, too." She studied Joe for a moment. "Did you find any gold when you panned with the other men?"

A sly look crossed Joe's face and he looked around him. "Why? You want gold for helping my leg?"

"No. I was just curious. It seems quite a lot of gold came out of that river. Did you know that?"

"No gold for white men. Gold for Chinese."

Nellie wasn't sure what he meant. "Are you living in Ketchum or Hailey? Where can we find you if we need to ask more questions about Hung Lui? Or the white men?" Or the gold, she said to herself. She wondered if Joe knew about the sacks of gold powder at the Vienna Mine that the sheriff had loaded into his automobile. Where was he?

"Berview. Other Chinese stay. River," he said, and moved his hand up and down. He stood. "I go now." He walked with a limp as he went to the door of the salon.

"Joe, who slashed your leg? Was it one of the men who panned for gold or one of the white men?" Nellie had followed Joe to the door of the salon. She lifted her hand to stop him and realized that might not be appropriate.

"White man who chase me. I fall. He cut." Joe accompanied this word with a swift downstroke of his arm. "I kick. He fall. I run away."

"Could you identify the man if we found him?" She doubted it was Bubba. He had seemed too round to run fast.

Joe shook his head. "No can do." He turned to walk away.

Nellie wanted to ask more, but Joe acted impatient to leave.

"You should rest your leg. See a doctor in Hailey."

The man set his face in a grimace. "No doctor. Ah Kee gone."

"Maybe stop at the sheriff's office. He has questions, too."

"I stop. No one there. Door rocked. No rights. He does not work." Joe gave that same swatting motion again. Flies, no matter, don't bother him, he seemed to intimate.

"Thank you for coming to see me, Joe High Sing. I'll show you to the front door."

As soon as her visitor left, Nellie hurried to the telephone in the kitchen. Goldie, of course, kneaded bread on the table. "What did he want?"

"Joe High Sing panned for gold in Smiley Creek and gave me the names of the others who were there. One man was murdered, and Charlie and I are trying to find the criminal." Nellie stood on the small stool to reach the telephone. She jiggled the holder up and down to get the operator to answer. "This is Nellie Burns. Please connect me to the sheriff's office in Hailey. Thank you." She waited. And waited.

Nellie hung up and turned to Goldie. "No answer. I'm getting worried. Charlie met Sammy and me on the road yesterday and then went to pick up a man at the Vienna Mine, one we locked into a cage in the mine adit."

Goldie sighed. "Charlie can take care of hisself, but I'm not sure about you." She pounded the bread one more time, then placed it in a bowl, a dish towel on top, and the bowl in a warm place in the kitchen. "Now don't you go driving back up there again."

"I can't. I don't have an automobile, and Henry is out somewhere. Besides, I am breaking my bank paying for gasoline. I need to buy an automobile, for cheap. Where would I look?" Nell sat down at the kitchen table. If she couldn't even buy gasoline, how could she afford to buy a motor car?

"Nothing around here is cheap. Go to Twin Falls or Boise. Maybe Gwynn Campbell has an old beater you could use. Farms and ranches usually have old broken-down machinery, including motor cars." Goldie opened the icebox and brought out eggs. She opened a drawer near the sink and pulled out flour, a measuring cup, and sugar.

"Now what are you going to make?" The woman was a baking maniac.

"Cookies." Goldie worked in silence with a sifter, a large spoon, and a dollop of Crisco. "Want chocolate bits?" She stopped her motion to look at Nell. Nell watched Goldie, but she was seeing something else. Hung Lui's body, the maggots, the bone. She shook her head to release the images and turned her attention to what Goldie was doing.

"What's wrong, little Nell? Don't worry. Charlie will be all right. He is a strong, smart man. I doubt if anyone could get the better of him."

"But who would try? He was picking up a hurt man who couldn't escape." Nell didn't mention that he carried several pokes of gold dust. There had been Bubba, Hank, and who was the third man? Maybe he had been with Bubba earlier and had returned. If two of them set upon Charlie, how would he manage? Surely, they knew better than to harm a lawman. Then they would be in big trouble, not just jailed for kidnapping Chinese that no one cared about anyway. Sorry, Sammy, Nell thought to herself.

"Seems to me Charlie Azgo has built up a bunch of enemies out of the criminals around this valley. Now, scoot. Go mope somewhere else." Goldie finished beating the batter in the bowl. "Oh, I almost forgot. A letter came for you yesterday. I put it on your desk in your studio."

"A letter?" Nell hurried back to the salon and searched the scattered papers she had mussed on her desk getting pen and paper for Chinese names. There it was. From her mother. She opened it with trepidation. Had her mother received Nell's letter about her engagement and with the invitation to come visit?

My dear Nell,
Your welcome letter arrived this morning and I am

writing back right away. I am so happy about your engagement because you sound so happy. I will come visit to meet your sheriff. Do you want me soon or wait until the wedding? I don't think I can come twice. I do not think the library would give me time off twice. Your loving mother.

"My mother is coming, my mother is coming," Nellie called as she ran into the kitchen. She wanted her here, now. What if Charlie didn't come back? Maybe the federal marshal had sent him somewhere far away. Maybe he lay hurt in the Vienna mine. Maybe he changed his mind about marrying her. Nellie looked at her ring. Goldie took the letter from Nell's waving hand and read it. "I want her here, now!"

"That won't happen, Missy. Go to the telegraph office. A telegram will speed up her trip. Sending a letter back will waste another four or five days."

Moonshine, who had been sleeping near the woodstove, drawn by the warmth, jumped up when Nellie came running back into the kitchen. He circled her and acted as excited as his mistress. "Guess what Moonie, your grandmother is coming to visit!" She covered her mouth. "Ooops, I don't think my mother would like to think of herself as a grandmother." She knelt to hug her dog. "Where's Henry? I need to borrow his auto to go to Hailey!" Moonie licked her face.

Nell stood and dashed out of the room and up the stairs to fetch a jacket and a purse. She would wait in the front foyer for Henry to return.

Chapter 14

SAMMY VISITED JOE HIGH SING in Bellevue. He and other Chinese lived in tents near the river after the caves where they stayed were filled in. Joe needed to visit the sheriff and Miss Burns to tell them what he knew, even if he lied about Hung Lui. Sammy went with him to the sheriff's office. No one was there. The sheriff should have returned from the Vienna Mine with the fat man, Bubba. And the gold. Sammy wanted his reward.

The cobbler finally agreed to loan his automobile after Sammy promised to share some of the gold dust. Sammy's mother said he was twice a fool. The sheriff deserved whatever happened to him after he took all the gold dust. He probably left the Big Wood River valley to turn the dust into gold coins. Now Sammy would never see any of it.

"The sheriff was engaged to Miss Burns. He would not leave her behind," Sammy said.

"Ha!" she said. "Gold will turn any man's head. It turned yours." Maybe she was right.

Joe said he would come, too. He wanted some of the gold, even though he escaped without turning anything he found over to the white men. First, they went to the jail to see if Bubba was there. He was not.

All the way to the Vienna Mine and ghost town, Joe said no

word. Sammy asked him if he wanted to see Hung Lui. He did not. They passed the sheep and sheepherder who paid no attention to their motor car. Sammy thought to stop and ask if he had seen the sheriff, but what good would that do? The sheriff did not return to Hailey. When they turned around the bend to the mine, the sheriff's auto was not there. Joe and Sammy waited to climb out of the auto, both looking around the area. The sun had sunk behind the mountain, but it was still light out.

"Basko sheriff come here?" Joe squinted.

"Miss Burns and I thought so. We told him Bubba was in the cage and gave him the keys." Sammy opened the auto door and stepped out. "Let's see if Bubba is still here." They walked up to the cage. The door was open, but there was a body pushed up against the wood frame to the adit. "Oh, oh." Sammy, the twice-a-fool, did not want to see who it was. He motioned Joe to look but he shook his head. Neither wanted to touch a dead body, especially a dead white man.

"We go," Joe said. "We go now." He turned and hurried back to the auto.

Miss Burns would hate Sammy if he left the sheriff there in the mine. He had to touch the body. Sammy picked up a piece of wood from the broken box where the gold dust had been stored and used it to poke at the man. A coat, one that looked like Bubba's, covered the head and shoulders. Maybe it was not the sheriff.

A groan. Sammy jumped, so startled. He thought it was Joe who had returned. Then Sammy realized it came from the man. He was alive. Sammy noticed the rope Bubba had used on him. It was tied around the legs of this man and maybe also the hands and neck. Sammy moved closer. The man's shoes or boots were gone. His feet wore only socks, and they were scraped and torn, as if he had run on rocks and dirt in them.

Since the man was not dead, Sammy touched him and pulled off the coat. It was the sheriff. Bruises covered his face. His shirt was ripped to pieces and his arms looked black. His hair, black anyway, appeared stiff with blood. How he was alive, Sammy did not know. He undid the ropes and called to Joe to help carry him to the auto. He must see a doctor. He breathed, but it was shallow. So far to go. Maybe the sheepherder could help. Sammy wished his father was with him. His mother had told Sammy about plants, about water, about blood. She had pressed a satchel upon him, as if she knew he would need it. Sammy opened it to see what could help this man. Joe did not care.

"Where auto?" Joe asked.

"Whoever damaged the sheriff took it," Sammy said. "Help me lay sheriff out on ground. I need water. Find some." A cup was in the satchel and Sammy gave it to Joe. There was also salve in small metal holder with a label in Chinese, "Bark for wounds." The sheriff's head still bled slowly, so Sammy used his bandana to press on the wound. More groans. Joe brought water, so Sammy cleaned off the blood and rubbed bark salve into the wound on his head. Much hair.

Sheriff's eyes opened. "Sam." Pain leaked from his eyes. "Hand." He lifted his arm. His hand was broken and his fingers wrecked. "Men pulled me behind…"

"Anything else broken?" Sammy felt along the sheriff's legs and other arm. On the wrist of his broken hand, the skin was red from a rope burn. Sam rubbed the salve on the burn. The sheriff tried to sit up. "No. We will put you in our auto and take you to Stanley." Then Sammy remembered only an animal doc lived there. No good.

The sheriff shook his head. "Alphonso. Sheep." He closed his eyes. Maybe passed out again.

"Joe, help me with sheriff, place in auto. Careful. His hand is broken. He is in pain."

"White man. I no care." But Joe took care with the legs, and they moved the sheriff to the auto. It was a small auto, but they managed to sit him up. He groaned but did not cry out. Sammy wanted to look for the sheriff's auto, but there was no time. Maybe the white men shoved it over a cliff with the sheriff in it. No, he said the men pulled him, so they used the auto to break him up. Sammy was glad he did not bring Miss Burns.

When they reached the sheep, Sammy stopped the auto and climbed out. At the end of the meadow, he saw the sheepherder and waved his hat. At first, nothing. Then the sheepherder mounted his horse and rode to the auto. He shooed dogs away. He saw Sammy was Chinese, but he slid off his horse.

"What is the matter?" He looked into the auto and saw the sheriff. "Charlie! Sheriff! What happen?" He almost climbed in, but Sammy stopped him.

"Sheriff is hurt bad. Head, hand, feet, arms. Maybe more. Can you help?" Sammy doubted the sheepherder could help. Then he remembered Miss Burns. He had helped her last summer. "Do you have a bed for him? I need to get a doctor."

The sheepherder shook his head. "Too far for doctor. I help where I can. Bring him to sheep camp." He pointed to the wagon near the road. Sheepherders used their wagons for sleeping, eating, living outside all summer.

Joe and Sammy moved the sheriff into the sheep camp and onto the bed across the back. Sheepherder—Alphonso—picked green herbs and soaked in hot water. Then he laid herbs across the sheriff's arms and feet and wrapped them up. He tied small splints on the sheriff's fingers and splinted his wrist, so his right hand straightened out. Sammy gave the sheriff a piece of wood to bite on. He thanked with his eyes. Joe sat outside in grass and fell asleep. Charlie slept again. Alphonso looked at his head and Sammy showed him the salve he had used. "Bark. Chinese." The sheepherder nodded and did nothing more there.

"What should I do now?" Sammy asked. The Spanish man was used to tending sheep. Better than the animal doc in Stanley. By now, it was getting dark outside. "Take the sheriff to Ketchum?"

"Let him sleep, so body heals. He is strong man. I tend to sheep. You and other Chinee wait here, please. Watch Charlie." He eased his shoulders. "I have lamb stew to eat for all. Charlie needs food and water." Alphonso left the wagon, and Sammy heard his horse move away. Sam did not know how to round up sheep or how long it would take. He stood at the double door and watched until it was too dark to see. Joe came in and said he was cold. Sammy lit the fire in the stove used to keep warm and to cook. Sammy tended Charlie and gave him water when his eyes opened by lifting his shoulders so he could drink.

"Sam." The sheriff nodded. "Rosy. Is he… with you?"

"No. Joe High Sing is with me. I can go get Rosy." Or Joe could, Sammy thought. But he was afraid to let Joe take the automobile. He might drive away and never come back. "We cannot find your automobile. Do you know where it is?"

Charlie shook his head and winced. "Might be above the mine. Men took it."

Sammy glanced around. Joe had stepped out. "Was the gold still in it?"

The sheriff opened his mouth and gritted his teeth. Then he closed his eyes and said, "I hid it. Men wanted it. Bubba dead."

In the middle of the night, an automobile came up the road, its

125

headlights bouncing up and down. Joe and Sammy slept under horse blankets outside. Alphonso kept a watch on Charlie inside. The sheepherder came out. He whispered, "Hide auto."

Sammy followed Alphonso's lantern and drove his auto behind the sheep camp. "Did you see the auto?"

"Yes. I do not know it. I know Charlie's auto." He sat down near the almost dead fire in the rock circle. He pushed embers to stir it and a small flame burst forth. "You and Joe hide inside." He picked up the rifle where it leaned against the wagon.

Sammy woke Joe up. The two of them climbed inside the wagon. The sheriff still slept, but the pain in his face had loosened. It was a sound sleep, not unconscious. Maybe. Alphonso gave him a powder mixed with wine after they all ate the lamb stew. Sammy helped feed Charlie with a spoon. He ate half a bowl full. The rest of the men ate a whole bowl each. No wonder Miss Burns liked the sheep camp.

Before long, the automobile came back down the road. It stopped where Sammy and Joe had stopped. Sammy heard a door slam and footsteps toward Alphonso.

"Hey there. Have you seen the sheriff—Charlie Azgo? Has he been around?"

Alphonso answered, "Who are you? No sheriff around here."

"I'm Rosy Kipling, the deputy sheriff. He headed up this way almost two days ago. He hasn't come back. Are you Alphonso, Gwynn Campbell's sheepherder?"

Sammy heard the relief in Alphonso's voice. "*Si*. The sheriff inside. He hurt bad." He opened the door and turned to the other man outside. "Two Chinese rescued him. They are here."

Sammy rescued the sheriff, he said to himself. Joe had nothing to do with it, but he did come. Sammy stood up from the stool near Charlie's bed. "I am Sammy Ah Kee. Charlie Azgo is here in the bed." Sammy recognized Rosy from his mother's house and at the bars in Hailey. Miss Burns said he stopped drinking and had changed his ways. He must have done to become a deputy sheriff. Also, he had helped Sammy move a body.

Chapter 15

WHEN ROSY BROUGHT CHARLIE BACK from the sheepherder's, he told Nellie what Sammy Ah Kee and Alphonso had done to save him. Rosy and Sammy carried him into Goldie's rooming house and took him to a bedroom on the first floor. Nell was sleeping at the time, but all the hubbub woke her up. She almost fainted when she saw Charlie. Goldie fussed around the room, trying to make it as comfortable as she could for Charlie. She had already called for a doctor to come from Hailey.

There was nothing for Nellie to do except sit beside him in a wooden chair pulled close to the bed and hold his un-broken hand. This was so much worse than the injury at Craters of the Moon.

"Rosy! Sammy! What happened? I was so afraid when his office was closed, and he didn't answer the telephone. Joe High Sing told me he was gone." Nellie wanted to hear the whole story. She had sent a message to Rosy, telling him she couldn't locate Charlie. Did Rosy know where he was?

"After you sent that message to me at Last Chance Ranch, I drove into Hailey to see for myself. I found Mrs. Ah Kee a-pounding on the door." He raised his eyebrows. Rosy did not like dealing with women in a tantrum of any kind. "I asked what she needed and she said Sammy went to Vienna to find Charlie and some gold." Rosy stopped and looked at Charlie. "Did you have any gold?"

Charlie glanced around the room. Sammy, Nellie, Goldie, and Rosy were there. Joe had left. He shrugged his shoulders and winced. "Nellie and Sammy gave it to me. I hid it. The men who did this," he said and gestured with his head down his body, "thought I had it. They found me at the cave and with the broken box."

"Did you let Bubba go?" Nellie had worried other men might have been hiding. She should have warned Charlie. She had thought Bubba was afraid of ghosts. Instead, he might have been afraid when she and Sammy took the gold that his partners in crime would accuse him.

"Bubba was dead."

"But—" Nellie didn't understand. The man had groveled, but he hadn't been injured except for his ear.

"Was he dead when you left?" Charlie had his sheriff voice back. Nell and Sammy looked at each other. They said "No!" at the same time. "He begged us not to leave him alone with the ghosts," Nellie said. "It was only later that I wondered if he really meant ghosts or something else." She turned to Sammy. "What did you think?"

"He meant ghosts. Vienna is a ghost town."

"The ghosts were real. They were men hidden deeper in the mine. They came out when I checked over Bubba. He had been shot. Real bullets." Charlie signaled he wanted more water.

"You're tiring him out," Goldie said. "Out. Out. All of you, except Nellie. The doctor is on his way."

"Goldie. I need to tell Rosy. He needs to find those men and Bubba's body." But Charlie closed his eyes and seemed to sleep again.

Nellie leaned over and kissed his cheek. "Goldie's right. I'll go and Rosy, you stay. When he wakes up, you can get the rest of the story. I'm not sure I want to hear it." She could hardly keep her voice steady. Her eyes filled, and she slipped out of the room with Goldie and Sammy. "All right, Sammy. You tell me." She hung onto his arm. He wasn't leaving without telling her what had happened.

"Joe High Sing told me the sheriff was not at his office. I borrowed the automobile from the cobbler. Joe rode with me. We drove to the mine entrance. The cage was open. A body lay against the crossed wood tunnel." Sammy's eyes widened. "I thought it was dead. I poked and it moaned. Then I knew it was alive. It had Bubba's coat over his head and neck. He was tied to the cage bar. When I saw it was the sheriff, we cut the rope and moved him to the automobile. Joe helped." His lips sneered. Clearly, Sammy disliked Joe.

"We took him to the sheepherder who treated his wounds with a green mess of plants and then bandaged him. I put bark salve on sheriff's head. In the night, Rosy arrived. He went first to the mine and then back down." Sammy shrugged his shoulders. "Rosy good sight to see. This morning, we brought the sheriff back. He is much better. My salve and Alphonso's herbs make him better. He still needs rest and doctor."

Nellie drew Sammy into her studio. "Why don't you rest on the davenport there, Sammy? I am so grateful you found him. Why didn't you get me to go with you? Why that man Joe? He accused you of murder."

"I found Joe High Sing in Bellevue. He told me about the sheriff's office and what he told you. I asked him to go with me. I am glad you were not with me. The sheriff was in plenty bad state."

Nellie nodded. She could not have stood seeing Charlie looking dead. Now, he was healing. "Did the men find the gold?" She knew it was important to Sammy, but she did not care a whit.

"Sheriff said he hid it. I don't know where. He did not reveal hiding place to the men, he said." Sammy's woebegone face pulled at Nellie. She knew Sammy wanted the gold to help take care of his mother. And send his father's and Hung Lui's bones back to China. Thank goodness, she did not have those worries. All she had to worry about was Charlie getting well again. His hand might never be the same. She was glad he was left-handed. The men who tortured him probably did not know his right hand held little power, even less now.

Chapter 16

NELLIE SAT WITH CHARLIE THE rest of the day, leaving only to eat a quick meal with Goldie in the kitchen. Rosy arrived in the early evening. He had left to go to Last Chance Ranch to check on his boys. His sister still lived with them, but Rosy worried about her. Her memory had been playing tricks on her, and he was worried she could no longer be responsible. "Tut," she told him, and he relayed that to Nellie.

"Rosy, we need to find the men who did this, Charlie's automobile, and the gold. Did Charlie tell you about any of these things? We are the law right now for Blaine County." It seemed a huge responsibility, but it would not be long before the citizens of Ketchum, Hailey, and Bellevue began to wonder about murderers in their midst. For all she knew, the Chinese might consider vigilante attacks on miners or miners might try to massacre Chinese again. The three men Rosy had taken to Boise may already have alerted the tong in that city.

"Has the doc come yet?" Rosy asked.

Nellie noted he didn't answer her questions about what he knew. Maybe she could get an answer from Charlie, if he woke up during the evening.

"Yes. He said Charlie needs rest, lots of it. The splints Alphonso tied to Charlie's fingers may have kept his hand from crippling up.

The cut in his head also is healing. It seems the sheep and Chinese remedies worked well. He did put a plaster cast on the sheriff's wrist, but that should repair, too." The doctor worried more about the man's feet than anything, although Alphonso's herbs helped fix them, too. Nellie remembered what those herbs had done for her arm.

"Then let's go, missy. We can take my motor car and head back up into the mountains."

"When? Not at night, surely." Nellie didn't want to leave Charlie yet.

"No. First thing tomorrow. I'll come on by and pick you up. Wear pants." With his bad eye, Rosy looked like a pirate. "Don't tell Goldie or Charlie we're leaving. And especially don't tell Sammy Ah Kee. It was all I could do to keep his mother from coming with me! We don't need a hysterical woman."

The doctor had left a potion to make Charlie sleep, but he refused to take it until late in the evening. "I want to talk with you, Nell. I heard you and Rosy talking. You should not go with him, but I know you will. Stop at Lulu's and get a revolver. I would give you my police gun, but it was in the automobile. Those men probably have it now, but no more ammunition for it." He had lifted himself to a sitting position. Nell held his good hand and had placed several pillows behind his shoulders. Charlie had always been the strong one of all the people she knew. Even stronger than Rosy. "Open the door." He gestured slightly with his head. "I want to make sure no one is out there listening."

Nell did as asked. No one waited in the hallway. She heard conversation in the dining room, normal laughter and a short argument or two. Goldie demanded they all keep it down because there was a wounded man in the house.

"Everyone is in the dining room. I'll bring in some food when they leave." She attached herself to his hand again. "Tell me."

Charlie seemed to change the subject. "Do you remember I was a sheepherder once?"

"Yes. You and Mikel talked about that when we were in North Idaho in Mullan at the Basque boarding house. Gwynn mentioned it a time or two also." Gwynn's description always included the word "damn" in front of it. Nell sat so she could watch the hallway. The men's voices in the dining room had quieted.

"And you stayed in Alphonso's sheep camp last summer." Charlie moved his plastered arm back and forth, as if it hurt.

"Yes. I remember that also." Why didn't Charlie just tell her what he was leading up to? He must have hidden the gold in the sheep camp somewhere. That would have put Alphonso in real danger, if the men who beat on the sheriff had any idea he had done so. Would Charlie have done that?

Goldie walked into the room carrying a tray with dinner on it. "This is for your patient, Nell. You go into the kitchen and eat yours. I'll sit with him." The landlady placed the tray on a small table near the bed and shooed Nellie out with her hands.

Nellie looked at Charlie. He gave a slight nod of his head. Maybe he was tired of her being there all the time, so she left. She could hear Goldie talk and Charlie's deeper voice as she walked down the hallway to the kitchen. She had already figured out that the bed Charlie lay on was Goldie's. Her landlady had taken over directing Charlie's convalescence, who was allowed in and who was not, and giving medications, including Sammy's salve.

When Nell finished eating, taking care of Moonshine with a short walk in the dusky evening, and returned to Charlie's borrowed room, he was sound asleep, and Goldie had disappeared. The tray no longer sat on the table. The kitchen sparkled and the dining table had been oiled. "Darn," she said to Moonie. "Now how do I get the information I need? Do you suppose he talked to Goldie?" Moonshine yawned and nudged Nellie toward the stairs.

* * *

The morning pulled Nellie awake before it was full light. Rosy had not said what time he would arrive, but she figured it would be early. She pulled on the pants she had purchased while in north Idaho, grabbed her jacket, the pack with her camera, and her wallet, decided to take Moonshine, too, and hurried down the stairs. Goldie met her.

"Now you be careful. I telephoned Lulu. She'll have a weapon for you, one Charlie said would be best. You know about the sheep camp," she said, just as one of the rooming house's miners appeared behind Goldie's shoulder.

"Breakfast ready yet?" He was one of the men Nellie didn't know well because he was new to the house. Henry brought him in a week or two earlier and Nell had been gone often, exploring old mining areas.

A nod to Goldie would have to suffice. She took Moonshine and left by the front door. Indeed, Rosy already waited. "I'm bringing my dog this time. I should have had him earlier." She pushed Moonie over the seat to the back, and he lay down and promptly dozed off. This was the automobile the three of them plus the dog had used to return from north Idaho. Moonshine must have thought it was another long trip.

"Doubt he'll be any use 'cept to bark and warn the murderers and auto thieves." Rosy grumbled for a while.

"We must stop at Galena, Rosy. Lulu has a revolver for me. Charlie and Goldie arranged it, as near as I can tell."

Rosy nodded, apparently not surprised. "About time. What with you runnin' off all the time, you need some kinda help." He looked over his shoulder. "Besides that there dog."

"You or Lulu will have to teach me how to use it. In spite of what happened in the Stanley Basin, I do not know how to use a gun." Nell had decided not to tell Charlie or Rosy about holding a gun on Bubba and firing it into the dirt. Besides, Sammy had taken it back and placed it—now that she thought about it, she wondered what happened to it. It would be dreadful if that was the revolver that killed Bubba. She would certainly be blamed. If they ever found him, that is.

"How is this going to work, Rosy? Do you have a plan in mind? I'm worried about running into what might be murderers." Nellie hugged herself. At least this time, she wasn't alone. And Rosy was, after all, the deputy sheriff. "If we both have weapons, that will help." She faced Rosy. "Do you have a weapon?" She had never seen Rosy carry anything but a bottle in the past. Thanks heavens, that wasn't a problem anymore.

"Charlie had me get a revolver from his office. I ain't much good at shooting a small gun like that, though." Rosy chuckled. He lifted his arm and made a gun shape with his hand and pretended to shoot. "Maybe we both need some practice time at Lulu's. She's got a target set up in back for the rubes she sells guns to. She might could teach us how to shoot." He gave a small *whoop*.

When they pulled up to the Galena Store, Lulu sat on the porch in the sun. There were no other automobiles, so Nell hoped she would have time to assist Rosy and herself in the art of the gun.

Revolver. Whatever. The pines all around the store gave off a heady scent of green.

"Howdy, folks. I heard you were comin.' I've got just the revolver for Nellie. What about you, Rosy? You armed?"

"Darn tootin' I am." Rosy brought out a gun that had been in his belt around back. "I don't know how to shoot it, though. Can you give us a try out?"

"You probably need a chest holster for that thing," Lulu said. "It must be awful uncomfortable tucked in back like that." Lulu reached for it and hefted it in her hand. "Big thing. Do you have ammunition?"

"Some. Charlie was about out of it, and his police gun got stolen. The ammo for that won't fit this one. I'm used to a shotgun or rifle for huntin.' Not one of these things."

Nellie left Rosy and Lulu talking. She let Moonie out of the car, and they walked around to the back of the store. There was indeed a target set up near an outbuilding and the corral. She felt anxious about handling a firearm. Her arm still ached from firing off that revolver of Sammy's up at the Vienna Mine. What was she getting herself into? She was not actually a deputy. She was a photographer. Which reminded her: she wanted a photograph of Lulu and the store, maybe inside and outside both. After she had sent the photographs of the saloon-keeper in Wallace to the Chicago newspaper, they had printed it and asked her for more, plus an article about the Wild West.

Lulu and Rosy came out the back door of the store, Rosy with his weapon. Lulu handed a revolver to Nell. It was not a cannon, like Rosy's resembled, but not a lady-size either. Lulu told Nellie how to hold hers. How to check for bullets in it. Then she passed her a small handful. "Never point this gun at anyone, unless you plan to use it," Lulu warned. "Once this gun is in your hand, it is a weapon and could be used against you. When it is not in use, keep it unloaded and locked away." Nell nodded.

"Hold your arm out and use your left hand to hold your right hand steady. Aim at that target." Lulu gave directions in a low, firm voice. "Fire."

The revolver exploded with sound, just like the revolver of Sammy's that Nell had fired. This time, she didn't have the same ricochet action. She peered at the target. "Which one is mine?"

Lulu laughed. "See that hale bay over there. You got it sure." She motioned for Rosy to come near and had him line up his revolver as well. "You know how to shoot, 'cause you've hunted. Hold this one steady and squeeze the trigger."

Rosy and Nell worked at loading their weapons and shooting them until they could do a passable job, according to Lulu. "Now, be careful. Try not to get into any gunfights. Just use these for protection. On your way."

Although Rosy had an underarm holster, Nell had nowhere to carry her revolver. Finally, she decided to put it in her pack until she needed to have it handy. But then what? "Lulu," she called as the store owner climbed the back stairs. "Where do I keep this... revolver when I'm not shooting or hiding it in my pack?" She held it out. "I mean, if I want to use it but not yet." The smell of gunpowder in the corral had covered up the pine scent in the air. Nell wrinkled her nose. "And how do I clean it?"

"We ain't got time for that now," Rosy said. "We'll come back later, Lulu. In the meantime, I know how to clean guns." He stuffed his gun into the holster and motioned to Nellie. "We got to get going. Round up that dog, and let's head up to Vienna."

The back route to Smiley Creek looked all too familiar to Nell.

"If Sammy and Joe didn't see Charlie's automobile, the bad men must have taken it down a ways, at least. There were a bunch of side roads that didn't look used. Maybe they hid it in one of those. They didn't dare drive it around. It has a police badge on the sides." It was another sunny day, There had been no rain for days and the dust rose as their automobile passed by. "All this dust! Someone can see us coming from miles away, I bet."

Rosy scratched his head. "Pretty curvy. I doubt the dust can be seen up ahead. Maybe I better slow down, though. Last thing we want to do is run into 'em and surprise ourselves."

"There's the gold, too. I think it is at Alphonso's camp, but I don't know where. Did Charlie tell you or at least give you a good hint? He seemed reluctant to say while he was in bed at the rooming house." Nell had tried to puzzle out what he was going to tell her. The sheepherder's outfit was the same one Alphonso had occupied the summer before in the Stanley Basin. She pictured it in her mind: the wagon bottom, the curved canvas top, the bed and woodstove inside, the drawer—aha! That big drawer under the bed held a myriad of camp tools, clothes, a rifle, pots and pans, everything Alphonso needed for the summer.

The miner had geared down, slowed the auto, and Rosy pointed to a side road. "Let's try up there. Not so much grass in the middle of this road." He turned the wheel and the auto bumped over ruts, rocks, and holes for a first section and then settled down onto a smoother section of gravel. The road headed up the side of a mountain, and the side grew precipitous within five minutes after they had turned onto it. The bank leaned down into a chasm.

"Stop," Nellie said. "I want to look over into that drop-off. Sammy suggested the men pushed the motor car over a cliff." When the auto stopped, it tilted slightly towards the edge of the bank. Nell climbed out and stepped to the edge to look down. Moonshine followed her. They both looked over the edge, but Nell could only see bunchgrass, weeds and rocks. She decided to walk forward and keep looking down. Moonie followed her footsteps but kept his nose in the air. What did he smell, she wondered?

Rosy had stepped out of the auto, too, but he leaned across the top, waiting for Nellie to return. She walked perhaps one hundred yards to a wide spot in the road. Still nothing to suggest anyone had been along the road in a long time. Back at the auto, Nellie said, "There is a possible turn-around spot up there. I don't think there is anything along here. Let's go to the sheep camp. Charlie talked about it before we were interrupted, so I think he might have been telling me to go there." He never actually said that, though. Nellie thought the sheep camp was too obvious a place to hide gold. She was sure Charlie wouldn't want Alphonso to be the next victim of those terrible men who killed Hung Lui and now Bubba. She continued to feel guilty about leaving him locked up. Charlie had been right behind her and Sammy. It didn't take long for Bubba's "friends" to get there.

As they approached the meadow where Alphonso kept his sheep camp, she could see it was empty of wagon, sheep, horse, and Alphonso. He must have moved during the night. Maybe that was what Charlie tried to tell her. Nellie didn't know where the sheep and camp would have been taken. The one big meadow was where she had always seen them. "They must have moved, Rosy. Let's go on to Vienna, but slow way down as we approach."

"When we get there, why don't you dig out your camera and take photos of the ghost town while I snoop around? Then maybe anyone there will just think we're tourers." Rosy presented this proposition to Nellie as they rumbled along the dirt road.

Rosy shifted gears to speed up for the next stretch of road but slowed again when Nellie motioned with her arm. She and Sammy had parked at least one bend before the tumbled-down village, but still, they had been attacked by Bubba at the mine. Even so, she suggested Rosy pull the auto into a half-hidden location. They climbed out and walked with Moonshine by their sides. "Don't bark, Moonie. We need to be quiet."

At the town, Nellie pulled out her camera and tripod. She wanted a photograph of the miners' boarding house. Then maybe the saloon, but she didn't want to go inside it again unless Rosy and Moonie went with her. "Rosy, don't get out of shouting distance from me, please. This place makes me nervous. There may not be ghosts, like Sammy said, but strange men use this as a hideout of sorts, it seems."

Rosy nodded. "I ain't never been here before, so I'll just wander around for a bit and keep an eye on you. If'n you see something you don't like, just call my name."

Nellie had brought a filmback so she could take several photos without re-loading every time. She tried to select the most complete buildings or the most interesting of the fallen-down structures. The sun shone on her activities and the warmth of the day began to heat up. The silence weighed heavily on her activities. Her peripheral vision caught Rosy several times, but then she realized she hadn't seen him in a while when she finished her last photo. She wanted another one or two at the mine and to investigate whether the road continued up from there. Moonshine had poked here and there as well but seemed mostly content to stick close.

Her camera still stood on the tripod as she walked a few steps up the once road in town and looked around for Rosy. She didn't want to call out as so far, she hadn't seen anything she didn't like or anything suspicious. She thought she might have seen a face in the boarding house window, but the half-collapsed building would have been a difficult place to stay. Moonshine uttered a low growl and Nellie spun around. An unfamiliar man strode toward her.

"What do you think you're doing here?" He had a country accent, even a southern accent, one not familiar in Idaho. His hair was blondish and he might have been good-looking except for a straggly beard. Maybe he was the one she saw when she followed the trail to find Sammy, now days ago, maybe weeks ago. Time had slipped out of joint when Charlie was hurt.

"Visiting and photographing. What are you doing here?" Nell hurried back to her camera and began to remove it from the tripod.

"None of your business. This here's private property. No trespassing." He motioned with an arm as if to say, "Scram."

Moonshine stepped between the man and Nell. He again growled, but made no motion toward him, although he continued to move closer to Nellie.

"This is a town—Vienna. The mine may be owned, but I doubt if the town is." Nellie wanted to back up, but she needed to get her photography gear together and out of harm's way. "The map I am using came from the Forest Service."

"I don't care where it come from. You are trespassing. How'd you get here?" Up close, the man's beard hung in strings and had food on it. His hat had holes and might have been worn while digging in the mine. Dust and cobwebs colored it beige, but it appeared to have once been blue felt.

"That is none of your business. You can't kick me out of the townsite. How did you get here?" Her hand slipped down to Moonshine and she held him by his collar, waiting to see if she should let him loose.

"Why, you—" The man grabbed the camera from Nellie's arms and jerked. He lifted his arm high and dashed the camera to the ground. At the same time, Nell released Moonshine, who jumped on the man with a loud snarl.

Nellie screamed. "My camera! Look what you've done!" She dropped to the ground to retrieve the pieces—the bellows, the lenses, the shiny wood panels. "Oh, no!" She glared up at the man. When he moved to strike her after he shoved Moonie off himself, she snatched up the tripod and swung it around, trying to protect herself. "Rosy, Rosy!"

The man raised his foot and smashed it down onto the wood panels and lenses, breaking them into shards and scraps. The tinkle of glass could have been her heart breaking.

Moonshine lunged again and grabbed at the pants leg of the attacker, snarling and growling. The dog might have known how precious Nellie's camera was to her. All his efforts were too late.

Rosy came running down from the mill, his face flushed from the effort. "Stop! You crazy man! Stop!" He ran up to the stranger and knocked him over like a bowling pin. He pounded at the man's face and neck. Grunts and moans came from the pile of the two men. Moonshine barked and Nellie screamed.

The noise and dust surrounded Nell. She tried to reach the pieces of her camera and could not. Finally, she sobbed. "Stop! That man broke my camera!" The melee calmed down. Rosy stood up and so did the man, each panting and sweating. If ghosts haunted Vienna, surely they would have appeared in the midst of the fight.

Rosy pulled handcuffs from his jacket. "You're under arrest, mister. Assault and battery. Damage to property." He moved toward the man. Dangling the cuffs.

"You can't arrest me. She attacked me first." The man took off his filthy hat and slapped it against his leg. "Look what her dog did!" His pantleg was torn and blood seeped from his lower leg.

"I'm deputy sheriff around here." Rosy flashed his badge on his shirt by moving his jacket aside. "Now hold still, you criminal, or I'll shoot ya." He had pulled out his gun when the man cleaned his hat. Then he handed the gun to Nell. "Keep it aimed at his head until I get him cuffed."

Nell took the gun. She wished she had her own revolver because she had at least practiced with it. It still rested in her pack, the pack now empty of her camera. She held it aimed at the man while Rosy twisted him around and cuffed his hands together behind him. Then he took it back. "Now go get the automobile. We'll hook him to that while we check out the rest of this town." Rosy turned to the man. "Anyone else around here? If you lie, you'll pay for it."

"N-no."

"Are you Hank?" Nellie asked. "I think I've seen you before. Only then, you carried a machete." He might have been the man who slashed Joe's leg when he chased the Chinese gold panner whom Nell helped in the camp near the river.

From his surprised look and then his glance to the side, Nell surmised that she had finally found Hank. She thought he was the one who said Hung Lui had drifted from Smiley Creek down to the Salmon River and then to the ocean. She remembered it was Bubba who said he hoped Hung Lui was slashed and that the Chinese man had recovered and run away. And now it seemed as if Hank was the one who might have killed Bubba with a gun. "Pat him down, Rosy. He might have a gun on him." She backed away. "I'll go get the auto. Be careful."

Nell walked as fast as she could down the road, calling to Moonshine to go with her. She couldn't stop thinking of her camera. It was like losing her best friend. All the shiny wood panels. The keen packaging of the bellows and lenses. What would she do without it? What would she be without it?

At the automobile, she circled it and checked to be certain no one had tampered with it and that no one was inside it. She flung her pack into the boot, but pulled her revolver out and, like all the men, tucked it into her back belt, keeping her jacket loose to hide it. Awkward to get it out, she guessed, but didn't know where else to put it. She hoped she didn't shoot herself. She gathered some ammunition as well and slipped the bullets into her jacket pocket.

When she drove the automobile back into the old town, Rosy stood with his revolver aimed at the man Nellie thought of as Hank. There was another man standing separately from the two—deputy and captive. Rosy and the man spoke together. Nellie noticed his longer dark hair hanging below his hat but didn't think she knew him. His cleaner dress than most of the men she'd come across up in the Basin made him appear to be from a city. Then she recalled where she'd seen him.

"You're the fisherman," Nellie said. "What are you doing here? And where's your fishing gear?" She glanced around. "Where is your automobile?" She couldn't remember exactly what he had been driving when he passed her and Sammy and the sheriff.

"I'm Dean Baker. I left my fishing gear up there." He moved his chin toward the road leading to the mine entrance. "Are you a deputy, too?" He stepped toward Nellie with his hand outstretched.

145

She ignored him. "Secretive men, aren't they?" Nellie stepped closer to Rosy.

"I don't know this man that the deputy has handcuffed." The fisherman stared at Hank, who kept his head lowered. All the fight seemed to have left him. "I'm a stranger in these parts, just looking around and seeing some of the old mining works. I heard this was a good one to visit because some buildings were still here along with a mill."

"You saw the mine entrance? See anything there?" Nell held Moonie's collar. She thought it a little strange that her dog hadn't growled or moved away from her side. If this man was as innocent as he pretended to be, Moonie would have gone up to him and sniffed. He did neither.

This Dean Baker wore no beard, but he did keep a hat on his head. Two fishing flies decorated the brim. His face was tanned close to the same color as his tan jacket, which was buttoned part of the way up. His shirt was open and chest hair sprang from the top. Gloves covered his hands. New boots covered his feet. He might have waded in them, but his pants showed no signs of having been wet.

"I just walked down from there," Baker said. "Funny mine entrance with that cage attached, don't you think?" He looked around, as if seeking something in the town, but kept his hands hanging at his side. "I didn't go in—it looked dangerous. You two been in there?" He looked first at Rosy and then at Nellie.

"Let's put this criminal in the back seat and drive up there. I ain't never seen it, and I hear interesting things took place." Rosy pushed Hank toward the automobile.

"You need any help?" Mr. Baker asked Rosy, who shook his head.

"You just go on looking around. Never know what you'll find in these old buildings." Rosy snickered. "You find any gold along with fish back down the road? This Vienna mine coughed up a bunch of gold back in the day. Then it went bust."

Nellie again tried to pick up pieces of her camera. Some of the wood panels survived Hank's stomping feet, but none of the glass lenses did. It was a total loss, just the way she felt.

Chapter 17

THE MAN HANK ENTERED THE back seat of Rosy's auto without complaint. Rosy kept the handcuffs on him and tied a rope from his hands to the gear shift, creating what appeared to be a most uncomfortable position for his prisoner. Still, Hank said nothing. Nell watched the man Baker, who studied the situation but did not comment. There was something about him that she didn't like, but she could not figure it out. Why would she dislike a fisherman?

"I'll walk up," Baker said. "I can always come back and hike around the town."

Rosy glanced at Nellie. She wanted Baker gone, as the deputy apparently did, but there seemed no way to stop him. Nell tried her best to remember the third man she had seen early on when she looked for Sammy. Could this be him?

The short drive up the road took no time. There was an auto there and it looked familiar to Nell, although she couldn't name the maker. "Let's follow the road higher, Rosy." She wanted to find Charlie's auto. Maybe they would learn something from it. The road wasn't really a road, more a track perhaps used at one time, but not for a long while. Weeds, grass, and rocks hid tire tracks except in one spot where water lingered in a mud puddle. Nellie motioned Rosy to stop, and she jumped out to study the mud, even drying from the heat of the day as they neared it.

Moonshine, who had been sitting near her legs, jumped down, too.

"Smell anything, Moonie?"

The dog sniffed around the puddle and lifted his muzzle to look at Nell. She took it as a signal to bend near him. She touched the mud. She could see and feel a tire track, but what was clearer was a footprint! She studied the track and followed it where grass turned to mostly rocks and pebbles. Something had been dragged up the mountain side. Not something—Charlie.

Through the auto window, she could see Hank peering at her. They stared at each other, and Nellie knew as clear as she was standing there that he—Hank—did this. His face flushed and he dodged her gaze. He began shouting at Rosy to let him go. He had done nothing wrong. This was illegal and on and on. Nell walked around to Rosy and he lowered his window.

"Charlie's footprint is over there, along with a tire track. Look up that way." Nell pointed, ignoring Hank's laments. "You can see where something was dragged through the rocks and weeds. It looks like a chute. Charlie is not a small man. This looks like when the sheepherder was dragged behind a horse last summer." She could hardly keep her voice steady. Tears filled her eyes, but she turned away and wiped them. The injury to her camera, which could be replaced, was little compared to the injury done to Charlie. "I think Hank did this. He probably shot Bubba, too. I'm not sure how that Dean Baker figures into this, but it is certainly coincidental that he showed up here just as we did."

Rosy opened his door and stood up. "Speak of the devil," he said as he watched Baker come up the track.

"I wondered where you all went to," Baker said. "Is there more mining up this road? It's hardly a road, though."

"Never been up there," Rosy answered. "Pretty steep for this here automobile." He put his head back inside and said to Hank, "Shut your mouth or I'll put a gag on you. I can hold you now for attempted murder." He stood up and Baker's mouth had fallen open.

"Murder? That's a far cry from property damage."

"None of your business, Mr. Baker. Just keep going up there if you've a mind to but leave the law business to us." Rosy waved his arm to encompass Nell.

Baker looked like he couldn't decide what to do. When he kept walking, Nell climbed back into the auto. "Follow him. He might lead us to Charlie's police auto."

When Rosy started the motor and crept up, Baker turned around. He had unbuttoned his jacket, Nellie noticed. She pulled her own revolver out from her waist band, just to have it handy.

"Mister, they're gonna shoot me!" Hank yelled out Rosy's window. Baker walked back to the auto. By then, Rosy had his revolver out and lying on his legs.

As Baker neared the window, he stopped. "I don't want to be any part of this." He turned first one way and then another. "I'm going back down. I hope you two know what you're doing. If that man in back doesn't show up in Hailey, I'll report both of you. I happen to know the sheriff." He buttoned the middle button of his jacket, glowered at Rosy and Nell in turn, and walked down the road. He didn't look back. Nell kept her eye on their prisoner to see what he would do. If Baker was part of the trio she had seen, Hank must be shocked at being left alone.

"Why, that—" Hank cut off whatever he was going to say. "I'm going to charge you with false arrest and kidnapping." Then the man sat on the middle hump on the floor and rested his head on the seat. A single drop of moisture trailed down his cheek. Nellie wondered if it was a tear or just sweat. She could feel sorry for him, but not quite.

"Let's go up past that bend," Nellie said. "This road is so rough and steep, I wonder if any automobile can get up, but the police car should have been able to handle it." She patted Moonshine's head and neck, feeling the comfort of his black hair. He rested his chin on her leg, maybe sensing her need for affection. She was pretty sure she wasn't cut out to be a deputy.

Around the bend sat what they were looking for—the black automobile with the police badge on the door. Charlie's auto. "So, they pulled Charlie behind the auto, maybe both up and down this godawful track. No wonder he was in such bad shape. They left him for dead, that's for sure. Then stashed it up here, thinking no one would find it until they came to get it and drove it somewhere away from the Stanley Basin and the Big Wood valley." Rosy left his auto and bent near the police bumper. "Look, you can see the rope he was tied to." He turned to yell at Hank. "Consider yourself lucky, you criminal, that I haven't tied you to my bumper."

Rosy circled the automobile and opened one of the doors to peer in. "The key is in here." Nell also ducked in to see if all seemed normal, and it did—except for the smell. No longer did Charlie's scent of leather and lanolin from his sheepskin coat hang in the air. Instead, the dregs of something liquid, maybe booze of some kind, and spoiled food, hung like a heavy fog. It felt as if someone was living in the machine. In back, a crumpled blanket or rug lay on the seat. There was a wire barrier between the front seat and back, the better to carry malcontents or prisoners. "Maybe this is where Hank has been staying. Better shake out that rug, or whatever it is." Nell didn't want to touch it.

Rosy pulled open the back door. "Whew. Stinks in here." He

grabbed the blanket and shook it. Nothing fell out. "I'll put our man in here and take him back to town. You drive my auto down."

Nell nodded. "First, let's go back to the mine and look around. Maybe we should try another side road if we see any, possibly to find out where Alphonso went. I'd hate not to find the gold while we're up here." She closed the door on her side. "I want to make sure that Baker man left, too."

The two of them transferred Hank to the sheriff's auto where his cuffs were locked onto the screen. His ride down would be slightly more comfortable than in Rosy's automobile. And Nell didn't want the responsibility. She might shoot him for destroying her camera if he acted up at all.

At the mine entrance, both Rosy and Nell entered the cage. Its door stood open, bent somewhat at the top end. The wood barricade inside at the actual mine entrance had been broken and lay in pieces. Hank's handiwork again? Nellie stood in front of it and tried to see deep into the tunnel. She could see little, but the smell of damp soil, metal and sulfur assailed her, taking her back to the mine in North Idaho where so much had happened. She backed away. "I'm not going in there."

"Me neither. We got our fill of mines already." Rosy hefted one of the wood cross beams. "We should put a barricade back up or lock that cage." He walked the space around the entrance, leaning low to inspect the broken box. "Bet the gold was in here, don't you think?"

"Yes, that is where Sammy found it. There were several leather pouches—a little like the ones in Last Chance Ranch. But these carried gold dust and nuggets. They were heavy." Unlike the lavender and opium button-filled pouches Nellie had discovered at Rosy's ranch house. "We left Bubba tied to that barricade. I wish we'd taken him with us when we left."

"No sense cryin' over spilled gold," Rosy said. "He might have overcome you and Sam on the way down." He kicked at the splintered box and hit his toe on a metal tool. He grabbed it up. "Huh. This must be what busted up the barricade." It was a pickaxe. "Heavy. Would make short work of that. And maybe of Bubba, too."

"Charlie said he'd been shot." The thought of anyone using the axe on a man made her shudder. "Do you suppose he is down that tunnel somewhere?" She would leave him there if that was where he was.

"Dunno. I'll do what I can to put up the barricade, and then we should tie the cage door closed. And then let's get goin'."

Nellie followed the big black automobile that Rosy drove. Moonshine had snooped around the entire area while they worked to close the barrier and the cage. He seemed happy enough to enter Rosy's auto where Nellie sat in the driver's seat. Mr. Baker's auto no longer sat near the mine entrance, so she presumed he had left the area. Back in the ghost town, Rosy slowed down and crept past the derelict buildings. Nellie saw nothing to remark upon. She and Rosy had decided on a signal—a brief horn tap—if one or the other wanted to stop and look at anything.

About a mile or so down the road, Rosy tapped his horn, and his arm came out his window, signaling a turn to the right. Nellie had never noticed any kind of road in that direction, but apparently he did. She followed him. They bumped along another wagon road in tandem as it climbed through aspen and evergreens. Eventually, it came out at another high meadow snuggled up against a rock wall. They both exited their vehicles and Rosy stomped around. "There," he said. "A sheep camp."

Nellie followed the deputy. "Yes, that is Alphonso's, but I don't see him or any sheep. Where could he be? Even his horse is gone." If the meadow was close to the rock face, the camp appeared to be part of it. Rosy had sharp eyes. "Let's go over and see what we can see." For a moment, she glanced at their own vehicles, but decided to leave them be, and Hank as well. Since no dogs or sheep were around, Nell let Moonshine walk with them.

Their route took them over bunchgrass and through a few sagebrush and even more bitterbrush. Alphonso must have known about this meadow from his own meanderings around the area. As they neared the camp, Nell commented. "I wonder where he's gone. The sheep probably ate most of the grass around here, maybe earlier, but Alphonso must be returning or his camp wouldn't be here. Let's go in. He never locks it up." Nellie climbed the three steps to the double door. She turned the handle. It was locked. She turned to Rosy in surprise. "He never locked it last summer. Maybe he was worried about the men going to and fro to the mine, although we are some distance from the road." Then she whispered: "Or the gold is in here."

Rosy joined her on the step. "It's a two-part door. I'll try to push the top in." He heaved his shoulder against the wood. It creaked, but didn't move. Moonshine had joined them on the step. He crooned a sound when Rosy hit the door panel.

Nellie stepped down to be out of Rosy's way. "Come down, Moonshine. Let Rosy try again, but then let's leave it. I don't want his camp to be broken. I wonder he even had a key." One more try, and the fastening on the inside gave way, letting the top swing open. "You are strong, Rosy." Much more than he looked, Nellie thought. All the years mining gave him more than one kind of strength.

Inside, they could see that everything had been turned topsy-turvy. The drawer in the bed had been pulled out and dumped on the floor. The cans and bottles above the wood stove had been smashed, and rice, flour, beans, and coffee spilled to mix with everything else on the floor. Potatoes had rolled under the chair and various herbs peppered everything. Their heady aromas combined to make a potpourri concoction. Moonshine stayed outside, maybe upset at the smell.

"Oh, no." Nellie hung her head. "Someone looked for the gold in here, undoubtedly. Poor Alphonso. What a mess!"

"Don't think they found anything. Otherwise, the search would've stopped. Looks to me like everything was tore apart. No guns either, so Alphonso maybe planned to be away and took everything valuable."

Including the gold? Nellie wondered. She couldn't stand the mess, so stepped outside and sat down on the steps. Maybe this was the last straw: Hung Lui, Joe, Charlie, Hank, her camera, the mine adit, and now Alphonso's summer home. She felt like crying, but what good would that do? Nothing. Then she heard pounding on the police auto window. Hank yelled, based on what his face looked like, but all she could hear was pound, pound, pound. "Rosy, you'd better see to your prisoner. I'd just as soon shoot him." Her revolver sat safely in the automobile she had been driving. Maybe she'd better get it. Who knew if the person who trashed the sheep camp hung about, waiting to see if Alphonso showed. A gunfight at the sheepherder's camp was all they needed. Her dog growled at the noise from the police vehicle, but he didn't go close to the machine.

"I'll at least fix the latch I broke," Rosy said, as he sidled by her. "I'll see what that jerk wants. Why don't you give a walk around. Maybe there's some clues."

Nellie could almost hear the quotation marks around "clues." Nothing on the outside of the camp looked disturbed. A black frying pan and deep kettle were hooked on one side, along with curled rope, a crowbar, a sagging water bag—empty most likely, a container of dog food that was half torn open with biscuits spilling out. No dogs around. Alphonso took everything with him except cooking tools. He must plan to return. She continued her walk around. There were no horse tracks, no tire tracks that she could see. Whoever had come probably sneaked up from the road, but how did they know the camp was here?

Rosy returned with his canteen. "He wants water. Anything in that bag there?"

Nellie pushed at the bag. No water sloshed, but it felt heavy. "No, maybe we'll have to get some from the creek. I could use some, too." She tried to lift the bag. "Rosy, shhh." Nellie glanced back at the police auto. Hank no longer pounded on the window. "The bag is heavy," she whispered. "Take it down, but pretend it isn't heavy, more like an empty water bag. I think the gold might be in there." She studied the ground beneath. There had been water there, maybe spilled earlier, but the puckered dust was now dry. "Put it in my auto and I'll go to the creek. Give me your canteen, too. You stay and watch here. I could use something to put the gold into, if that is what it is."

With another quick glance at Hank, Nellie tripped up the stairs and into the mess in the camp. She found an empty bottle, unbroken, and came out with it. "I'll use this as a separate bottle for your prisoner. You don't want him drinking from your canteen. Who knows what kind of germs he carries." She followed Rosy to his auto and opened the door for him. He swung the bag in as if it weighed nothing. She hoped it did, and she was right about its contents. "I'll go down to the creek and get back right away. I'll leave Moonshine with you to help guard."

One creek had followed the main road, Nellie recalled as she slowly back tracked. Once she turned on the road, she found a likely spot to place the auto and get water. Before opening the boot, she glanced up and down the road. Seeing nothing, she lifted the water bag, heavy indeed, and placed it in the boot and covered it with a rug. Then she took the bottle and the canteen and filled them both. Back at the auto, she was put out because she hadn't brought a top to the bottle. Oh well, she thought, she could carry it on the seat beside her.

Back at the sheep camp, she handed both the bottle and the canteen to Rosy. "I spilled some and didn't see anyone or anything moving. Any sign of Alphonso?"

Rosy shook his head but pointed back from where Nellie had come. "Looks like we got company. You get back in my automobile and turn it around and head out. This guy is like a bad smell— can't get rid of him."

Indeed, it was Dean Baker again. She hoped he hadn't seen her move the water bag to the boot of the auto. "All right, I'll turn around, but you do it, too. Where is Moonshine? I want him with me. Don't wait to fix the door. I'll drive slowly, but if you don't show up soon, I'm coming back." When Rosy scowled, Nell added, "I don't want you beat up like Charlie was. If Baker and Hank are in this together, they could cause as much damage to you as they did to him. For all we know, they attacked Alphonso, and he is lying out there somewhere." That thought made her shiver. Surely, the sheepherder was all right, or his dogs and sheep would have been close by, waiting for him. "Where is Moonie?" She hurried to the auto she was driving, calling for him and waited to climb in. "Moonshine!" Her dog rushed up and climbed across the seat, and she sat down. As if she hadn't seen Baker, she backed and filled to turn the auto around, but then drove in the meadow around him to get out the track, although he had tried to stop where she couldn't. She waved and kept going, bumping up and down on dirt and uneven ground. She noted when he stepped out of his auto and waved at her, that his jacket was completely off this time and no holster was in sight. Maybe he was just an innocent bystander.

At the road, Nell headed down the mountain, but kept her foot on the brake. Moonie jumped into the back seat and then again into the front seat. He was as nervous as she was. She was just turning around again to see what the hold-up was when she saw the police auto come out of the track. She breathed a sigh of relief and then saw that two people rode in the front seat, and one of them didn't appear to be Rosy. She waited until it came even with her and saw that Baker drove and Hank sat beside him, his hands still apparently cuffed.

"What are you doing? Where is Rosy?" Her voice was short and stiff, she knew.

"That deputy wanted to go find your sheepherder, so I said I'd drive Hank down and hold him until he came in my automobile." He moved his head toward the prisoner. "Show her your cuffs, mister."

Nell couldn't remember if she had ever called the prisoner Hank in Baker's hearing. She studied both men. "I don't believe you. I'm going back to see where Rosy is. If you've hurt him in any way, we'll catch you and you'll pay for it." She gunned her engine and drove up the road to the track. She noticed in her mirror that the police auto didn't move. Her revolver still sat in her front seat.

She thought about shooting it to blow out a tire or a window, but her aim was definitely not that good.

Her own auto bumped along the track again as she hurried to find Rosy. She wished Alphonso were close by and could help. Two men against an old deputy and a young woman weren't good odds, but at least they were armed, or she was. Moonshine made a good weapon, too. Three against two.

Chapter 18

SAMMY AND JOE HAD STOPPED to see the sheriff where he lay in the bed in Goldie's rooming house. Then they headed to Hailey. Joe wanted to go to Bellevue, and Sam had business with his mother—Chinese business. He did not want Joe around.

In Bellevue, near the entrance to the woods by the river, Joe climbed out of the automobile. He turned to duck his head to get the last word. "Good thing I was with you, Sammy. You would have had a hard time all alone." He glanced around, maybe to be sure no one heard him. "I am sorry I accused you of Hung's death. That Miss Burns said 'anyone who knows you could not think you did it.'" He nodded. "She right." Then he stepped away and slammed the door. Sammy was glad to be rid of him.

Since Sammy was already in Bellevue, he decided to visit the caves where the Chinese lived for a while until the owner of the ground filled them in. He parked on the space above the drop-off where the caves had been. The wood stairway hung broken. Word was someone fell there and hurt himself or died, and the owner of the land kicked everyone out of the caves. Sam took a deep breath and decided he would be careful going down the stairs rather than slip on mud down the slope. It was almost dusk and no one else was around.

At the bottom, when Sammy jumped off the last step, he could see the caves had been filled in, all except a shallower one, only scooped out, maybe a separate cave in the first place. He scrambled around the rocks, piled dirt, and brush to peer in. It was not just scooped. A half-tunnel had been dug in a ways. Sam wished he had brought a lantern. There was nothing to do but return to his mother's house to get a lantern and maybe a shovel. He could see something toward the rear of the dugout.

Sammy's eyes almost closed with tiredness as he headed back to Hailey. His mother worked in her kitchen, only a sideboard of sorts, to combine powders to make a concoction. "What are you doing?"

"I am repairing a problem that is none of your business." She stirred and carefully poured the concoction into a small jar. Then she added a small amount of liquid, stoppered it, and shook the jar vigorously. "What do you want?"

"I need a lantern and a shovel. I cannot find the shovel. Did you hide it?"

"Why would I hide a shovel?" She continued to shake the jar.

"Because you used it and either lost it or did not want me to know you used it." Sammy sat down on a bolster near their rolled sleeping mats. All he wanted to do was go to sleep.

Mother held the jar up to the light above the sideboard. Satisfied with the color or thickness, she placed the jar near her herbs and powders. "It is done." She slipped on a jacket that hung nearby. "I am going to deliver this potion while it is still strong. Wait for me. I will show you where the shovel is."

"Good. Then you can come with me." There was no question as to where they were going in his mind. She slipped out the door. Sammy laid his head on his sleeping mat.

Sam's mother shook his shoulder. It was completely dark outside. How long had he slept? When had she returned? "I will come with you, Sammy. I will show you what I have done. Get up."

The shovel and a lantern sat beside the borrowed automobile. He must return it to the cobbler. After, he thought. After. The cobbler knew Sammy would return it as soon as he did not need it anymore.

When they entered Bellevue, his mother instructed him to take a turn to the west. "This is a better way of getting there."

How did she know where they were going? Sammy did not know, except his mother knew many things and felt many other things. Sammy knew this about her. They turned again onto a muddy track and soon reached the once-caves.

"This is where you take me, true?" She opened the automobile door and closed it quietly. "It is better if others do not know we are here."

This felt almost like the night Miss Burns and Sam had accompanied his mother to the grave of his father, the empty grave. He had known then that his mother had removed his father from under the earth, so that his bones would appear faster. She had done to him what Sammy had done with Hung Lui. Nature would take its own course.

"Take the shovel and loosen the box. It is full. Bring it out here. Here is the lantern." Mother held the lantern. Sam took it and the shovel, and crawled half upright into the dugout. He worked at the box and loosened it from the earth surrounding it. It was good he had slept a little while. He was not so sleepy. He knew what he would find. The smell now was the damp earth and wood of the box. A heavier smell, not quite one he could identify, held back. He pushed the box with his feet and the shovel until he was outside.

"Here," his mother said. She lifted the lid and there were his father's bones. They shone white in the moonlight and lantern light. She knelt and whispered in Chinese to his father. When she stood, most of the lines in her face had smoothed out. She leaned over and lifted what Sammy first thought was a rock. It was not. It was his father's skull. There was a break in the skull where a hatchet had killed him. Sammy and his mother knew who or rather what had done that. Opium.

"Did you scrape the bones?" Sammy asked his mother. He knew many Chinese had performed such a chore when men had died on the railroad work, and tradition required them to send the bones back to China. He shuddered but tried not to.

Mother lowered her chin but kept her eyes on Sammy. "I knew you would not."

"Put the lid back on. I will carry the box to the auto and I will send off the bones as soon as I can. I wanted to wait for Hung Lui's bones to go at the same time, but they are not ready." She continued to hold the skull. Sammy lifted the box. His father had been a large man, but the bones were not heavy. The lid slipped askew when Sam stumbled on a hidden log. A gibbous moon shone down on them—a man, a woman, a box of bones. They shone white. They were ready. Moon bones.

*   *   *

By the light of the moon, Sam Ah Kee carried the box to the automobile he had borrowed from the cobbler. He stowed the bones in the boot and then realized his mother had not followed him. "Mother? Where are you?" He kept his voice low, knowing she did not want others to find them. No answer, so he returned to the dugout. He needed to pick up the shovel and lantern. Neither the tools nor his mother appeared before him. A noise inside the dugout caused him to step to the entrance. "Mother?" A faint light shone from the back of the space.

"I am here." Her voice wavered, conjuring an image of a ghost to Sam.

"What are you doing? Come out now. It is not safe in there."

"I don't want all of my beloved husband to go back to China. He is mine."

Sam remembered his mother had still held his father's skull when he moved away with the box of bones. "We can talk about this. Come out and bring my honored father's skull. Being buried in a dugout in Bellevue, Idaho, is not the place for him, either."

Her voice moved closer. "Don't send my bones to Guangdong. I hated it there. I want his head with me." Closer still. "His spirit will just dally with his old wives in China. He wanted to be there, but he cannot have everything. Without his head, he will still be mine."

Sam heard scraping. "Mother, what are you doing? I will do whatever you want. You are my honored mother."

The scraping stopped. "No, Ah Kee was your father, but someone else was your mother. We stole you away. That 'friend' of yours, Hung Lui, knew the secret. That was why he had to—" The sound of rocks and dirt tumbling cut off his mother's voice. And then there was nothing. No voice. No mother. A last chunk—rock or dirt—tumbled and then no sound.

For a stunned moment, Sammy stood still. Then "Mother! Mother!" he shouted. He tried to shovel with his hands into the dirt pile that now closed off the dugout. His mother! His mother was buried.

A shadow approached him and then two more. "What are you doing?" came a question.

"My mother is buried! We must get to her!" Sam continued to scrabble at the clumps of dirt and rock. "Help me!" He heard murmurs behind him. After what seemed a long time, a shovel appeared in someone's hands. He grabbed it and began digging, making headway this time.

Another voice. "Sammy Ah Kee! What are you doing here?" It was Joe High Sing.

"My mother is trapped. Help me!" Sammy kept digging and an arm appeared and the others around him finally believed he was not crazy, and he was not digging for a ghost.

Someone pulled his mother out from the dirt and tried to get her to breathe. Sam crouched and pulled dirt out of his mother's mouth. Her face, white and drawn, had no life in it. Her other arm circled his father's skull, still resembling a piece of stone. He pulled at the head to put it aside, but her hand would not release it. Others helped him lift her body and take it to their automobile. "I will take her to the hospital. They can revive her." They laid her in the backseat, murmuring she was gone, she was not alive, her ghost would be following. He knew it was true.

At the hospital, a wood-sided house, no one would even allow Sam and his dead mother inside. "No Chinese allowed!" The night duty caretaker pushed Sam away.

As he trudged back to his automobile, a small woman followed him. "Let me look at her." She opened the rear door and checked over his mother's body, taking care and handling her gently. "She is gone and there is nothing to be done. Take her to the morgue at the butcher's shop in Hailey. I will try to ring him up. Tell him the night nurse sent you." She looked up at Sammy. "I am sorry. You should let the sheriff know, too." She dashed back and closed the door.

Chapter 19

NELL DIDN'T KNOW WHAT SHE would find—Rosy injured or dead? When she reached the high meadow, she jumped out of the automobile. Moonie followed. She saw no one, heard nothing but bird song. A breeze pushed the grass all in one direction, like water flowing. Again, no sheep and no dogs. No Alphonso. Baker's automobile sat to the side. She walked over to peer in and saw fishing gear.

The sheep camp. She climbed the small stairs and pushed the door open. Rosy had not fixed the latch inside. The same mess greeted her, although the single drawer had been reset under the bed and a half-hearted effort to re-fill it showed someone cared about what happened there. Was that Rosy? Where was he? Moonshine nosed around the mess and stared up at Nell, as if she were responsible for it. He turned and walked out the door and down the steps.

"Where is Rosy, Moonshine? Can you find him?" She followed her dog outside. Moonie nosed around and then paused, looking toward the meadow. Even Nell could see a faint trail, as if someone had walked through it. "Wait. I have to do something with the water bag in case Baker comes back." She glanced at the track, but it was empty. Maybe he had gone on down the road. Maybe he hadn't lied. She wondered why Rosy would not have detained Baker. Maybe with a "false arrest."

Nell opened the boot and lifted the heavy water bag. She needed to fill it again with water, but then it would be too heavy to lift to where it usually hung. Still, she managed to hook it to the side of the camp. She found the jar that she had filled at the creek. It was now empty. Maybe there was a smaller creek in the woods. "Water, Moonshine. Find water." Her dog turned from staring at the meadow and trotted to the woods. He disappeared in the trees and eventually, she heard an *Arp*.

With another jar she found in the camp, Nellie followed Moonie into the woods. He lapped water from a small tributary, large enough to fill both jars, and she carried them back to the hanging bag, Moonie at her side. She stood on a wood round, one Alphonso used with an outdoor fire ring, and poured the water through the top fastening. Soon, the bag was half full. Enough, she thought. No auto had yet followed her track to the camp. No Rosy or Alphonso had appeared either. Moonshine's ears perked. He heard sounds, sounds too far away for Nell to hear. She stood at the meadow and listened. Then, she, too, thought she could hear the baaing of sheep, a low rumbling in the distance. The blue sky was empty of clouds, so not thunder. A dog barked—a sharp, insistent sound. The sheep and dogs! They must be coming.

"Moonshine, I have to put you back in the camp or the auto. Where do you want?"

Moonie walked to the automobile and sat by the door.

"I'm sorry." Nell opened the door and he jumped in. "If Alphonso sends the dogs into the meadow, I can let you out again."

Soon, a horse with two riders appeared at the far end. It must be Rosy and Alphonso. She waited while the trio came toward her. One of the riders slid off the horse and continued to walk her way, while the horse and rider paused to watch the sheep. A whistle sounded and the sheepdogs rounded the animals to a compact bunch. Several continued to browse, but the rest settled into a woolly group. The grassy lanolin scent carried on the breeze to the camp.

"Why are you here, Missy?" Rosy called to Nell. "Didn't that son-of-a-gun Baker tell you what we were doing?" He removed his hat and slapped it against his leg. "Damn dust."

"He did. I thought he was lying, so I hurried back to see if you were all right." Relief welled up inside. Rosy was his usual cantankerous self, the one she liked best of all.

"I couldn't leave that criminal here while I looked for Alphonso. He was sneaky enough to escape and maybe get the gold. So I bargained with Baker to take him down to the trailhead. He left his fancy auto here as hostage. I'll meet him down there." He plopped his hat back onto his hair, which was turning pepper and salt and plastered to his head in the heat.

"I guess I understand why you let him take the police car, but I wouldn't trust him as far as I could throw him."

"That's why I wouldn't let him go down in his own automobile. It's a far sight nicer than that police wagon. Fair trade if he skips out."

Alphonso walked his horse up to Nellie and Rosy and tied the reins to the camp. "Alphonso, I am so glad you are all right, too! Did you plan this with Charlie?"

The sheepherder grinned. "Good plan. They looked everywhere but didn't find the gold." He gestured to the water bag. "Gold comes from water. It can stay in water. No one finds."

"I did," Nellie said. "But only because our prisoner needed water." Water was already dripping from the bag. They were lucky the men who searched the camp had not seen the tell-tale sign. "I'll help you clean up inside, and then we must get back to Hailey with the prisoner, if he is still around." She glanced at Rosy.

"Never you mind, Missy. So far, we can't prove anything but that he broke your camera."

The sheepherder frowned. "Your camera? Oh, Miss Burns, I am *desolado*. You need your camera!" He shook his head. "That is much worse than mess in camp. I will clean. Rosy said he will get the camp tender out here with more supplies. With those men gone, I will be *muy* safe."

Rosy and Nell conferred. Rosy would drive Baker's auto and Nellie would continue with Rosy's. They prepared to leave.

"Is the sheriff o-kay?" Alphonso had lifted the saddle from his horse. "I worry about him, but he said to take sheep and camp away from other place."

"He was much better when we left early this morning. Alphonso, thank you for all you did for him. The green poultice saved his feet, the doctor said. He also said Charlie's fingers should repair fairly well." Nell moved to the sheepherder and hugged him. "You are the best doctor of all." She let go. "And Sammy's salve helped the sheriff's head."

"You marry him, yes?"

"Charlie," she said and laughed. "Not Sammy. He is too young for me."

"We might better take the gold," Rosy said. He lifted the heavy bag down and poured out the water.

"Do we know for certain the gold is in there?" Nell opened the top and felt inside. Her hand met the wet leather of the pouches. "Unless the gold was poured out, it is still there." She tried to lift one, but between the water and the gold itself, the pouch was too heavy. She shrugged. "Do you want to check it out?" she asked Rosy and Alphonso. Both shook their heads.

"I'm not so sure. How did the door get locked? The camp was searched inside, but then we found a locked door." Nell stepped up to the door and studied the knob, a round one with no fancy plate like in Goldie's house.

"Senor Campbell replaced the door last winter. He tied a... key to the—" he said and turned his hand, "and I just left it there. I knew I didn't need to lock anything up."

"All right. Mystery solved. Let's head on down the road, Missy. I don't want to give that Baker a chance to cross us up." Rosy swept his arm around, and Nellie gathered up her pack, empty of a camera. She felt a visceral need to photograph the door and the camp.

*   *   *

The trip down the road to Smiley Creek and its bridge took as long as usual. Nellie kept going over all the events in her mind, trying to figure out who killed Hung Lui, who killed Bubba, who ransacked the sheep camp, who beat up the sheriff and almost killed him. She tried to posit how Sammy could have killed his friend, and then placed Joe High Sing as the killer. The Chinese men had said a white man, but Sammy said a white man would use a gun. According to Charlie, it was a gunshot that killed Bubba in the mine entrance. Hank could have done that and also ransacked the sheep camp after he tortured Charlie at the mine. Any man who would stomp a camera as he did hers, she reasoned, could stomp a man without compunction.

Dean Baker presented an enigma. He seemed to be just a fisherman and tourer, catching trout and looking at sights.

Certainly, others had done the same around the old gold camps, including Custer and Bonanza. Vienna's access was longer and more difficult but not impossible. Stories about it floated everywhere, including the saloon in Stanley and around the dinner table at Goldie's. One of the Triumph miners said that log houses from Vienna had been moved down to Stanley and were still in use. Nell suspected that Baker knew Hank. Maybe they were in league. His sudden appearances were just too coincidental.

At the bridge, no police car awaited. Rosy climbed out of Baker's auto and came to Nell's window. "Humph. Maybe you've been right all along. I thought we were supposed to meet here and make the exchanges."

Nellie sighed. "When I saw them, Hank was in the front seat next to Baker. He appeared handcuffed, but that might have been a trick." All her ponderings had come to no conclusion, but the missing auto may have sealed the deal about Baker and Hank being joint criminals. "Let's go down the road toward the trailhead. That is what you mentioned to me. Let me go first, so if they wait there, they'll think I am alone and you are on your way."

"I dunno, Nellie. They might figger out you have the gold in your boot. Where else could it be?"

"I have Moonshine. He can take care of at least one. Don't stay too far behind." Nellie drove off and took the turn to head toward the highway and not Smiley Creek Lodge itself. She wasn't too sure of this course of action either. They nearly killed Charlie. They wouldn't hesitate to kill her dog. Or even her, although they might hesitate for a moment. She made sure her own revolver was to hand on the front seat. "Moonie, get ready to jump out."

As she reached the top of one of the swales, she paused her automobile. Down below was the police car, off to the left side of the road and not moving. She could not tell if the motor ran. A figure sat behind the steering wheel, but from the angle of the auto, she couldn't tell if there were another person in the passenger seat. She moved the revolver to her lap, checked to be certain a bullet was in place. She intended to shoot if she had to.

Nellie looked back and saw Rosy coming up the swale. She opened her window and motioned him back. She raised and lowered her hand, hoping he understood to wait. Once again, he climbed out and came to her window, crouching down when he saw the police car below. "Anyone in it?"

"At least one person. I can't tell if both are there or not. I'll drive down and stop to the back and across the road. If I see the other person, I'll lift my arm out the window, and you come down, too. Otherwise, I'll open my door and let Moonshine out and I will follow."

"Nope. You ain't gonna. I'll go down and do what you planned. If my arm comes out, then you come. Otherwise, wait here."

"If you get out of your auto, I'll send Moonshine down, but then I'm coming, too. We know what they did to Charlie."

Rosy guided the Baker automobile down the hill and stopped where he said he would. He waited and waited some more. At last, he opened the door and stepped out. Nellie opened her door and shooed Moonshine out. He dashed to meet up with Rosy. Nellie took her foot off the brake and let her auto drift down the swale until she stopped behind Rosy and climbed out.

"Only one person and he's slumped over the wheel. I bet he's dead as a doornail."

"Which one?"

"Can't tell. I'll go 'round and have a look-see. Keep your revolver out and ready." Rosy looked both ways on the road, as did Nell.

No other automobile or person was in sight, but there were trees close to the road. Someone could be hiding there. It felt like the typical summer day with blue sky, a few clouds, a soft breeze, small twittering birds in brush below the trees.

Moonshine had settled next to Nell. Then he followed Rosy to the driver's side of the police car. The deputy opened the door of the automobile. When he leaned in, the slumped body fell sideways half-way to the ground. Nellie waited a moment to see if he moved. It looked like Hank from where she stood—bulky and his shirt pulled out. "Deader'n a doornail" seemed an apt description.

Nellie joined Rosy. He peered into the backseat. No one there.

"Looks like he got the same treatment as Bubba, a shot to the forehead." Rosy stepped over the corpse, whose hands were still handcuffed, and pulled him away from the auto. "Baker kept his side of the bargain. He brought this criminal to the trailhead and left him here in the police auto. 'Cept Baker musta been the real criminal after all." After a glance around the area, he said, "Wonder where he got to? Still a hike to the main road. We better keep ourselves alert. Got your gun?"

"And now we have three automobiles. What do we do about Baker's? Did you search it after they left?" Nellie didn't like being out in the open when they knew the "criminal," as Rosy called him, might be watching them. He had no compunction about killing people. She wondered if he was the one who slashed Hung Lui's throat. The sight she had seen with Sammy thrust itself into her mind. It was easier to think of gunshots to the head, although the result was the same. Moonshine sniffed around Hank and then poked his head inside the automobile next to where Rosy stood.

"Guess we leave it here. I didn't look earlier, but I'll do it now. Why don't you begin the drive home? You've got the gold in that bag, as near as we can tell, and we should get it to the sheriff's office. You're probably itchin' to see that fi-an-ce of yours, too." Rosy grinned. This was the first time he had mentioned Nellie's intended. "Should be a fast trip, what with no picture-takin' to slow you down."

Nellie had almost forgotten the loss of her camera with all the upset over Alphonso, the sheep camp, and Baker and Hank. Maybe she could borrow money from the bank to order a new Premo. That idea lifted her spirits somewhat. "All right, but I'll wait until we both go through Baker's automobile. For all we know, he set a booby trap. Here, Moonie, you can help, too."

The three of them crossed the road and Rosy opened the driving door. "Nothin' in here, except my stuff." He opened the back door. "Fishin' gear here." Then the boot, but Rosy prevented the lid from coming up more than a few inches. "Be careful. See if that dog of yours smells anything."

Moonshine already had his nose in the air, sniffing. Nellie held his collar so he wouldn't get too close to the inside. She didn't want to lose him to a trap. She doubted Baker had time to do anything elaborate, but still, they couldn't be sure. He might have expected the deputy to search the machine before he drove it down from Vienna. Rosy stood to one side and let the lid up further. Metal bars, a crowbar, ammunition boxes, rope, a machete, and an extra tire littered the back. "Watch out, Nell!"

A crossbow strung deep inside let loose an arrow just as Nellie dove to the ground, still hanging onto Moonshine, who landed with her. "Omigod. He did. He set a trap!" She stayed where she fell. "Anything else that you can see, Rosy?" Her heart almost leaped out of her chest and slowly relaxed as Moonshine scooted closer to her. "I think I'll just stay here."

Rosy poked around the contents, still leaning in from the side. "Nope. Don't see nothin' else." But he kept up his search. "I think we need to take it all with us. Might be somethin' to pin the bad deeds on him."

Nell crawled to the side, taking Moonie with her, and then she stood up. "Where do you think he is? He could be watching all this, Rosy. We know he has a gun." The hairs on her neck prickled, as if someone stared at the back of her head. She turned in a circle, studying the surroundings. "Let's load up and get out of here. I don't care what happens to his fancy automobile. It can rot right here. Can we disable it somehow?"

"I don't know that much about how automobiles run. I just drive 'em. But we can jerk a few wires under the front hood and take that machete and ruin a tire or two."

"Better not. There might be something on the machete that tells us he killed Hung Lui. He was an innocent man. Bubba and Hank were not. They were in this together for the gold. Sammy's friend got caught in the middle."

To be sure, Nell opened the boot of the automobile she was driving to check on the empty-of-water bag. It still laid on the floor. She had been with it or nearby the whole time, but as she had told Rosy, she didn't trust Baker at all. Ghosts, slavers, gold all combined to set her on edge. Worrying about Charlie, seeing the dead Hank, losing her camera—these aspects of her day heaped the pile higher or dug the hole deeper.

Rosy took the crowbar and slammed it into two of the tires on Baker's auto. He moved the junk in back, with Nellie's help, into the police car, and then the two of them lifted Hank into the back seat. He wasn't stiff yet, but soon would be, undoubtedly before they reached Ketchum. No stop at Rosy's Last Chance Ranch this time.

With a deep sigh of relief, Nell started up Rosy's automobile and headed toward the main highway. Even climbing up to Galena Pass felt normal again, except no stops to take photographs. Even so, Nellie pulled off to look back at the Sawtooth Mountains and the Stanley Basin. Not taking a photo freed her to enjoy the scene and helped block the ghost town of Vienna from her mind. The police automobile followed her the rest of the way to Ketchum but kept going to deliver Hank to the morgue in Hailey.

Inside the boarding house, Nelly hurried to Goldie's bedroom where Charlie lay, but he didn't. The double bed stood empty and re-made with a colorful quilt on top, as if no sheriff had ever filled it with an injured body. Even the medicinal smells from Sammy's Chinese medicine and the doctor's lotions had disappeared.

"Goldie!" Nell called. "Where is Charlie?"

"My gosh, you are noisy," Goldie answered as she strode out of the kitchen. She, too, looked through the door into her bedroom. "I couldn't stop him. He was bound and determined to go back to work, even as shook up as his poor body was." She shook her head, tut-tutting all the way back to the kitchen. "You took your time getting here, Nell. Was the gold where Charlie said it was?"

"Charlie never actually said where the gold was, but we found it, we think." Leaving the bag in the auto was not a good idea. "Goldie, would you come help me carry something into the rooming house?" On second thought, she wasn't sure she should leave it here, either. "No, maybe I should just take it to Charlie's office. Is he here in Ketchum or did he go to Hailey?"

"Darned if I know. Don't know how he got there, either."

Henry, the retired miner, rounded the corner. "You lookin' for the sheriff? I took him to his office in Hailey. He said it was bigger and the cast on his arm wouldn't get in the way there." He lifted one arm with the other as if he wore a cast. "He wants his automobile back. Do you have it? I didn't see it outside."

"No. Rosy is driving the police auto." Nellie closed her eyes and thought she could fall asleep right there in the hallway. "I better motor to Hailey. Thanks, Henry." She wanted to ask him to drive her, but then she'd have to move the water bag and making explanations was too much. "I'll be back, Goldie. Maybe with the sheriff, depending on how bad he is."

"Don't forget. Your mama is arriving in a few days to Shoshone. You said you would pick her up there." Goldie turned to Henry. "Nellie may need to borrow your automobile again."

Henry nodded his head and wandered away to disappear up the staircase.

Once behind the steering wheel, Nellie sparked up. Seeing Charlie would energize her, as always. She hoped he stayed in his office and didn't try to go out to do law business. She would be relieved to unload the gold in the water bag. The sheriff could see it got to the right people—the Chinese and Sammy. That responsibility would be lifted off her shoulders. She could get ready for her mother's arrival, a daunting task in itself. How long, she wondered, since she had seen her mother. Almost a year and a half. Would her mother be as changed as Nellie was?

The sheriff's office was dark and the door locked. Now what? Maybe Charlie went with Rosy to the butcher shop morgue to drop off Hank. Nellie shrugged her shoulders to relax them and motored on to the "morgue." There, she found Charlie, Rosy, and Mrs. Ah Kee, with Hank lying next to her. Nellie was shocked to see Sammy's mother and hear the news that she had been buried in a landslide. Seeing Sammy right away topped her list of where she would go next. Charlie said to wait. Sammy had already come in to find out about the gold and needed a reward to take care of his mother's funeral.

Back at Charlie's office, Nellie asked the question that had been on her mind. "Does he want his mother's bones to go to China, too?" She couldn't imagine Mrs. Ah Kee being left out in the open for animals and insects to feed on her.

"He did not say anything about that." Charlie had helped carry in the empty water bag.

Nellie noticed he was not wearing his pointy-toed cowboy boots but something more comfortable. His feet must still hurt. As no one else was in the office, she hugged Charlie. He looked most uncomfortable. "Go back to Ketchum, Nellie. Rosy told me about all the doings up near Vienna. I am sorry I was not there with you. I am most sorry your camera was destroyed. Somehow, we will get a new one for you." He took her hand with his unhurt one and squeezed. "You were clever to find the gold. I hope Baker did not find it first. If he did, both he and the gold are probably a hundred miles from central Idaho and still going."

"All right, I'll go." She gave one last pat on his shoulder and left the office. Charlie expected Rosy to take him to his Hailey home and not back to Ketchum. The miner could stay the night before returning to Last Chance Ranch.

Nellie motored straight to the Ah Kee house near the river.

Chapter 20

SAMMY OPENED THE DOOR TO Miss Burns when she knocked. She told him she had seen his mother at the morgue because Rosy had delivered the man called Hank, who was no longer alive. She said he was one of the men who had imprisoned the Chinese she and the sheriff had rescued and then sent to Boise to be safe. She thought Hank and another man had killed Bubba and were after the gold hidden by the sheriff. The sheriff was recovering. She thanked Sammy for saving Charlie and bringing him to Ketchum.

Miss Burns might have talked all night, standing there on the front stoop. Sam listened to her and said nothing.

"We found the gold—Rosy and I and Alphonso."

Sam needed the gold for his mother's funeral, but even she would not want gold spent on her.

"Hank broke my camera into a thousand pieces." Nellie's lip trembled.

"Come in, Miss Burns. I will make tea for you—my honored mother's special tea." Her camera meant as much to Nellie as the gold had meant to him, maybe more. Sam had cried over Hung Lui. Why couldn't he cry over his mother? She had said she wasn't his mother. She did not want her bones sent to Guangdong. The butcher helped Sam wrench his father's skull from her grasp.

179

Her ghost must be desolate.

Neither Miss Burns nor Sammy spoke while he made the tea. She had already said what she came to say. Her shoulders sagged. Her eyes stayed downcast. She sighed. She wore sadness like a shawl, and it wasn't even her mother.

"What will you do now?" Miss Burns asked after she took sips of tea. "You and your mother were so close."

"I must find Hung Lui's slayer. His ghost is lost and alone." Sammy sipped his tea also. "When I send his bones back to Guangdong, the ghost can rest, but only if I find who killed him. I must avenge Hung."

"Tell me what happened to your mother."

The two of them sat in silence for a little while. At last, Sam described the dugout and his father's bones, how the dirt collapsed, and how Chinese who lived in the woods helped Sammy pull his mother out. His tears began to fall. Miss Burns left her seat to sit beside him. Sam told about the hospital who refused to even look at his mother and about the nurse who helped them. Miss Burns said nothing but placed her hand on his arm. When Sammy stopped his recital and his crying, she removed her hand and drank more tea. It was cold then.

"A funeral for my mother," Sammy said. "And then I will bury her here. I am not sending her bones to China. She hated Guangdong. She said no." Sam heated more water and poured more tea. "I will do what she wished. Then I will leave. Chinese not wanted here. I will go to Chinatown in Boise City."

"Is there anyone there who can teach you your father's skills with herbs and potions?"

No one wanted herbal medicines anymore because so few Chinese were left. "No. I do not want those skills."

"What will happen to your house?" Miss Burns stood and paced in front of the stores of herbs and powders. "And all of these? It seems a shame not to use them. At least take them to Boise."

"The house I will burn. It should not have survived the earlier fire when other Chinese houses burned. All Chinese should leave Hailey. It is too empty to stay here without Hung Lui and my father and mother."

"Sammy, I am so sad for you." Miss Burns's eyes filled with water. "Please do not leave without seeing me again."

Chapter 21

NELLIE PARKED HER BORROWED AUTOMOBILE in front of the McFall Hotel in Shoshone. Across the street, she walked back and forth at the train station. The train from the East had not yet arrived. A few other people waited as well, but no one she knew. At last, a whistle sounded in the distance. It was such a lonely sound. Nellie passed through the station onto the apron outside to watch for her mother. The engine steamed and the cars clanked as the train came to a stop. Several men alighted first and then, there was her mother, looking like a sophisticated Chicago denizen, short skirt, cloche hat, fur boa, heels on her shoes, and strings of pearls down her bosom. Nellie felt like a country bumpkin in her split skirt, hatless head, and utility jacket. She should have dressed up.

"My dear daughter! You look like a Western woman!" her mother exclaimed. Her flapper bob looked much more severe than Nellie's. Red lipstick colored her mouth. "Carefree and almost wild! Do you have a horse waiting outside?" They hugged each other.

"No, Mother. I have an automobile—my coach to take you to my Western town. Where is your luggage?" She kept glancing at her mother, surprised at her sophistication.

"There is only one suitcase, as I can only stay one week. I absolutely loved the train ride. I felt as if I were going to another planet most of the way here. How did you ever find this place?" She hung onto her daughter's arm as they entered the station to wait for luggage to be delivered from the train. "No wonder you love it so much. But don't you miss the city?"

"No, not a bit." Nellie felt tongue-tied. What was she going to talk to her mother about? She couldn't regale her with tales about ghost towns and dead men and gold. She even wondered how she was going to introduce her mother to her crippled fiancée. He had not returned to Goldie's, so it would be easier to plan the meeting elsewhere—maybe at Charlie's house in Hailey or at Last Chance Ranch with Rosy, Esther, and the boys around. She had already hinted as much to Rosy and Goldie to get their reaction.

As Nellie drove, her mother chatted away about Chicago. Most of the news and gossip by-passed Nellie, until her mother mentioned Professor Blake, who had visited her recently and encouraged her mother to come and see her daughter. Cal Blake, a full professor in mathematics at Northwestern, had been wounded during the race riots in 1918. Her mother had found him on a sidewalk, helped him up and to her apartment. A doctor nearby had bandaged the wound and warned Blake not to go out on the street again until he recovered, a matter of a week or so. It was then Nellie had moved home from her grandparents to live again with her mother.

"You know it was Professor Blake who found me my job at the library."

"Yes, Mother. He was also the one who gave me a camera, told me how it worked, and helped me set up a darkroom in the apartment basement." Her memories of that time sparked a smile. "He also found the internship for me at Scotto's studio." Which she had lost, Nellie continued to herself. She waited for her mother to say something, but she didn't. "Without Professor Blake's help, I'd still be in Chicago."

"When do I get to meet your intended?" her mother asked as Nellie pulled up to the boarding house where she lived. To Nellie's eyes, the large two-storied house appeared seedy, something she had never thought before. She was seeing it now as her mother might.

"Let's get you settled first. You can meet Goldie Bock, my landlady. I can show you my room. I doubt if any of the miners are around during the day. Do you want me to introduce you as Margretta?" It felt funny to use her mother's first name.

"That's my name, Sweetie."

Nellie knew she looked a lot like her mother, fairly short, oval face, pouty lips, and thick dark hair. She also looked like her father in some respects: gray-green eyes, heavy eyebrows, and widow's peak. Her grandparents had been German immigrants, bringing her mother and brother to Illinois. What happened to him? As a child, she had known him, but he headed west to find gold in the Yukon and never came back. Her father had been Scotch-Irish and prone to drunkenness, which was how he ended up on the streets. Nellie had identified him at the police morgue.

Goldie met Nellie and Margretta at the door. All the clutter that once sat there had disappeared—shoes, books, coats. Goldie had straightened the place up. She shook Margretta's hand and told her how much she enjoyed Nellie. Then the landlady took them up the stairs and opened the door to one of the small rooms in which no one resided at the moment. Nellie carried her mother's suitcase and wondered what made it so heavy. Shoes, probably. Her mother had a fetish for shoes. "Do you want to get refreshed and then join us for tea in Nellie's studio?" Goldie asked.

"Let me show her my room first, and then we'll come," Nellie said. Goldie's warm welcome was a contrast to her usual moodiness. "I put clothes hangers in that little closet. If you need more room, you can use the closet downstairs just outside my room." Goldie had never even offered that space to Nellie. "I'll see you soon." She left.

Nellie slung the suitcase on top of the bureau. Her mother opened the closet, sat on the bed, washed her hands in the wash bowl. "Where is the bathroom?" Her glance around told Nellie her mother had expected a little grander place to sleep.

"Down the hall, Mother. You'll get used to it. Even hotels in these towns have shared bathrooms. We are not the city." She slipped her arm around her mother's waist. "You can have my room if you like and I will sleep here. Come, let's go look at it."

So far, Moonshine had not appeared. Nell wondered if Goldie were keeping him in the kitchen. She wanted him to meet her mother.

"You only seem to have men friends here, Cora Nell. Your landlady is the only woman you have mentioned in your letters. Otherwise, it is the sheriff, the miner, the photographer, and a Chinese man. I can't remember their names, except for your fiancée, Charlie Azgo. That is such a strange last name. I did look up Basque at the library where I work. He is Spanish, I take it—or is he French?"

"Neither. The Basque live on the border of Spain and France but aren't really either. Their language is one few people understand and has no provenance in other languages. They have their own culture." Nellie opened the door to her room, which she had straightened and cleaned, knowing her mother was a stickler for order. "According to Charlie, the Basque discovered America long before Christopher Columbus did."

"This is such a nice room. It is so light and airy!" Her mother twirled around and then sat on the bed. "Yes, I think I will trade you, if you really don't mind." She gave Nellie a sly look. "Unless your fiancé slips up here from time to time."

"Mother!" Nell knew her face flushed red. That had never happened, although she had sometimes wished it would. Hence the blush. "He only came to my room once, trying to find a thief who stole some negatives." Even that memory caused her some heat as she remembered throwing him out. "I found the thief instead. It was Sammy Ah Kee, my Chinese friend, only he wasn't a friend then." That reminded her of Mrs. Ah Kee lying in the morgue. "Let's go downstairs. Goldie undoubtedly has prepared the tea and a few goodies." She slipped out of the room after her mother and closed the door behind her.

"Don't you lock the door?"

"Not since my camera was broken. There is nothing of value in there to steal, and really, there's no one to steal anything."

"Your camera was broken? I am so sorry. I know it meant so much to you. How did it happen and what will you do now?" She stopped outside the door.

Nellie didn't want to go into detail about the past week or two. "I'll get a new one." Somehow. "Do you want to visit the bathroom?"

Her mother nodded and walked down the hall to the room Nellie had pointed out. When she came out, Nellie noticed her mother wore red fingernail polish. Her gloves had disappeared, perhaps into her purse.

In Nellie's studio, Goldie had laid out several plates with cookies and small slices of pound cake. She brought in the tea and cups, all in chinaware with delicate flowers and a gold rim.

Nellie didn't remember ever seeing such fancy dishes. Goldie had removed her apron and wore a dark blue and white polka-dotted dress with a white belt. Her landlady frowned briefly when she studied Nellie's split skirt. Definitely, she should have dressed for the occasion, which Goldie and her mother both had done. This room appeared more modern since Nellie had turned it into her studio. No heavy furniture, good light, special lights for portraits. Nellie felt more comfortable.

"I think you should take your mother to meet Gwynn Campbell at his ranch," Goldie said. "An auto trip to Galena and the Stanley Basin might be nice, too. Margretta could see what beautiful country we live in. You might even see some sheep up there." She poured the tea as Nellie and her mother sat on the davenport. "Guyer Hot Springs might be a good visit, too. I could go with you there. We'll see Last Chance Ranch tomorrow when Charlie and Rosy will entertain us."

Entertain us? thought Nellie. Moonshine trotted into the room. "Moonshine!"

Her mother made a slight sound and leaned against the back of her side of the davenport. "Oh, dear, a dog. I'm afraid of dogs. Does this one bite?"

"Heavens no, Mother. This one is my very best friend. He has… taken good care of me." She might have said "saved." That would not be an appropriate word, since she had never told her mother of the various scrapes she had encountered. "And I of him."

In the morning, Nellie and her mother walked around Ketchum, which didn't take long as the town stretched only a few blocks. It was a warm day and somewhat dusty. Her mother wore flat shoes, but still dressed as if she were stepping out of a bandbox. Nellie had explained they would be going north of town for lunch and to meet Charlie, along with Rosy, her miner friend, and his sons and sister.

Her mother rolled her eyes. "Sounds like a lot of people. Will they think this Chicagoan is a gun moll or some such? I know how stories about Chicago have traveled."

Nellie laughed. "Well, I must say, they thought I was one at an early point. Even Charlie suspected me of some evil deeds." She wondered if her mother could tell she was nervous about this meeting. Charlie could be so stoic and stern. Her mother could be flirty and dizzy.

Henry, the retired miner, loaded Goldie, Margretta and Nellie into his automobile, with Margretta in front. He appeared to relish being next to a "city gal," as he called her. Moonshine jumped in back, maybe knowing Margretta would not have appreciated his company.

Nellie had spruced herself up. She didn't want to be a pale mimicry of her mother, and in a short dress, a colorful scarf around her neck instead of a hat, and a pair of her mother's fancier shoes, she thought she looked less country and more city, but not Chicago city. She wondered what Charlie would think. She even added a touch of lipstick at her mother's suggestion.

"Nellieeeee!" "Nellieee!" Matt and Campbell ran toward the automobile as Henry turned under the log entrance, now finished with a sign: Last Chance Ranch. Rosy had been sprucing things up, too. The sheriff's non-police auto rested off to one side and Rosy's automobile sat beside it. The lavender looked to be in bloom and its perfume scented the air when the ladies stepped onto the path to the front door.

The boys hugged her. She motioned to each in turn to introduce them to her mother. "This is Mrs. Burns, my mother. And this is

Matthew and Campbell." She placed her hand above each boy's head. "Rosy Kipling is their father." She managed not to twitch.

By then, both Rosy and Charlie had stepped onto the front porch. Nellie climbed the two steps and placed herself between them. "Rosy and Charlie, this is my mother Margretta Burns, fresh from Chicago!" She couldn't place her hand on their heads, so she gestured to each. "Charlie Asteguigoiri is my fiancée," she said as she placed her arm on his. "Ross Kipling is my friend and the father of these boys."

"I'm so pleased to meet you both. Cora Nell has told me so much about you." She almost simpered, and then surprised Nell by holding out her hand to shake the men's hands. "I doubt I can pronounce your last name, Charlie, so let's just go by first names. You too, Rosy. I know that is what Nell calls you."

"Well, you're as pretty as Nellie here," Rosy said, "and you two could be sisters—twin sisters!" He took Margretta's hand and didn't let go for a long moment.

"I am pleased to meet you as well," Charlie said. "Welcome to Idaho and the Wood River Valley. Nell and I hope you like it as much as we do." He shook her hand briefly.

Oh-oh. His quiet, impassive demeanor.

Goldie lifted her hamper of food. "Shall we eat out here or go inside?"

"The bees are pretty busy today," Matt said. "Let's go inside, and then we can show Mrs. Burns our fort down by the river." Campbell nodded. "Our fort!"

Rosy offered lemonade or tea and hurried about to set the table, which had been cleared of its usual detritus. The long room with a fireplace at the end looked less like a male bastion than it had since Rosy and the boys had moved in. Esther, his sister, waited inside and Nellie introduced her mother again. Esther preened and commented on Margretta's city aspects, as if she and Margretta had just both come from Chicago on the train. Margretta welcomed the lemonade and sat in a chair near a window. "I must admit, I am a little breathless in this altitude. Cora Nell didn't warn me about how high you all are." She patted a chair beside her. "Come sit by me, Charlie, and tell me about yourself."

For a fast second, Charlie looked taken aback. He took the offered glass from Esther and sat down next to Margretta. "What would you like to know? And may I ask you questions, too?" He smiled.

Maybe this would be all right.

Margretta talked most of the period before lunch and then into lunch. She told about her position at the library, where she and Nellie had lived, about Professor Blake and his assistance to Nell with her camera, about women's suffrage, about the exquisite tall buildings in the city. She shifted to talk about the coming presidential race between Calvin Coolidge and John Davis. No one could remember the name of the third-party candidate.

"What about the gangsters?" Goldie asked.

"Yes, tell us about Capone!" Matt inserted.

"Wait until you show me your fort," Margretta said. "Then I'll tell you some stories."

* * *

Nellie and Margretta decided to travel over Galena Pass and into the Stanley Basin the next morning. They borrowed Rosy's automobile. Moonshine insisted on coming. Nell wondered if her dog knew he would be needed. She was a little nervous about heading into the area where a "criminal" still lurked, although he might have left by now. Charlie had whispered to her that the gold was in the water bag, but not all of it, so Dean Baker might have extracted some and been interrupted. Or maybe Hank had done it when Baker wasn't around, and a bullet in his head was his reward. The water bag had not been so secret after all.

It was another blue-sky day with some of the early summer cottony clouds to the north. The winding road caused Margretta a few moments of feeling sick, so Nellie stopped the auto twice to let her walk around. The aspen leafed out in bright green colors, backed by the darker green of evergreen trees. Once they reached the pullout for the view of the long Sawtooth range of jagged mountains, Margretta seemed to get a second wind. She exclaimed over and over again about the beauty, and stark peaks, the same impression Nellie always felt. The trip down the other side caused less discomfort. Margretta asked to pull over at the Smiley Creek Lodge. Nell was hesitant to do so, leery of bootleggers, but she did it anyway. She wouldn't let Moonshine out.

Several automobiles sat in front of the log lodge. Nell walked with her mother inside to use the restroom. The mostly men who sat at the front bar weren't any of the bootleggers Nell had come to know the previous summer. Maybe there was a whole new crew, but these men and two women (at a bar!) looked more like tourists than locals. Maybe they were on their way up to the Fourth of July Creek and Lake to the dude campout where Nell and Pearl, the saloon girl, had ended up. That was when Charlie had arrested Nell. She had not told her mother that story and didn't intend to.

Outside, Nell watched a somewhat familiar automobile drive away, spraying gravel and dirt on its way north. She sorted in her mind through the various automobiles she knew while she waited for her mother. "That's the one," she said out loud.

"One what?" her mother asked. "Someone you know? What a cute place this is. Are they serving alcohol in there?"

"Yes, I know it. Get in, Mother. I'm going to follow it at least up to Stanley. The driver is a killer." She wished she hadn't used that term.

"Ha, ha, ha. You've taken my gangster stories to heart, Cora Nell. People may think of this as the Wild West, but they've never spent time in Wild Chicago!" She laughed again but settled herself in their automobile. "So far, everyone here has been nice as pie, including your Charlie."

Nell hurried away from Smiley Creek and steered her way up the road to turn into Stanley. She thought she had seen Dean Baker's automobile head in that direction. At the Stanley saloon/café, which almost felt like home to her, she saw the fancy Baker auto parked in front. "Stay here," she said. "If anyone approaches our auto, let Moonie out."

Margretta opened her mouth, perhaps to protest, but then shut it again. She glanced into the back of the auto at Moonshine, Nell's black dog. Nellie hesitated at the front entrance. Leaving her mother alone to chase a killer was not a wise decision. She turned briefly, saw Moonshine in the front seat, and turned back to the door. At least she could hurry and find out if Baker was in there.

Inside the saloon, Nell strode to the bar at the back of the room. Sam the barkeep greeted her. "How are you, Miss Burns? Did you get that Chin—Chinese man Joe High Sing taken care of? He was a gloomy kind of guy. How about the other Sam—Sammy Ah Kee? I saw Joe again a week or so after you and the vet took care of his leg. He stalked around here and then left again. Funny guy, that."

"Hello, Sam. Do you know a man named Dean Baker? His automobile—a fancy one—sits outside here. He is a dangerous man. If you've seen him or know of him, I will have to call the sheriff of Blaine County about it."

Sam rolled his eyes. "All that sheriff—Azgo, isn't it?—does is cause trouble around here. I'd hate to see him again." He finished polishing the beer glass he'd been working on. No one sat at the bar as they did at Smiley Creek Lodge. "Yeah, I know Baker. Slippery character. He's run up one big bill here."

"He stole some gold. He can pay." Nell looked around the café which was indeed empty. She strode over to the dark room off to one side where the not-quite-welcome customers sat, the Chinese and Negroes and probably Indians, too, if any were around. No one sat in that space, either. It was time to get back to her mother.

A long scream sounded outside. Her mother! Nell ran out the front door, Sam in fast pursuit. Her mother was being bundled into the fancy car, and it was Dean Baker who was stuffing her in. Nell quickly opened her own automobile door to let Moonshine out, and they both dashed around two empty autos to Baker's. "Let her go!" Nellie yelled. "Moonie, get him!"

Baker rushed around to the driver's side, slid in and reversed the auto, then again sprayed dirt and gravel as he drove off, heading out of the small town and up the valley road. Moonshine chased it briefly but came back to Nell. "I have to go after my mother, Sam! Find someone else to follow us and help me. And call the sheriff in Hailey, too. Do you have a gun?"

"Yeah, behind the counter. I'll follow you and bring it. Hurry now. He could be headed to the Seafoam Mining area. It's pretty much deserted these days." He ran into the saloon, turning back to shout, "The road turns to dirt about a mile on. He won't be going so fast on it. Lots of bumps and ruts."

Nell figured she was about five minutes behind Baker. Once the pavement ended, she could see his dust far ahead. He had slowed, but she slowed, too, or her teeth would have been shaken out of her head. Moonshine sat in the front seat with her. He would have to be her helper if she could corner the man. It would take the sheriff or Rosy two hours to get to Stanley, even driving as fast as he could. And she drove Rosy's automobile. She hoped Sam the barkeep would turn up soon.

The Salmon River was behind her, but the Valley Creek ran beside the road, sparkling in the sunshine. Soon the road began to climb. She had never driven this way, nor did she know where the Seafoam Mining Area was, although she had heard the miners around the dinner table at Goldie's mention it. It was like Vienna—deserted. Her mother had purchased an automobile map from the drugstore when they had returned from Last Chance Ranch the day before. She wanted to find all the places on the map that had been mentioned at lunch. What had she done with it?

The dust cloud ahead of her disappeared. Nell had been so busy worrying, she had lost track of Baker. He must have left the road. There had been several turn-offs along the way, but Baker had still been ahead of her. She stopped to see if her mother's bag sat in the front well. It did. Her own much smaller pack, which contained her new revolver, was gone. She grabbed the bag and rummaged through it. The map crinkled and she drew it out and spread it on the seat, nudging Moonie to get into the well. It took her a moment to find Stanley and then the road to Cape Horn. In tiny print, Seafoam Mining Area was noted to the north. They had passed a shaded track not far back. Nellie turned her auto and crept along the road, looking for any kind of sign for Seafoam. At last, a hand-made sign with SMA on it pointed up one of the side roads. No dust to follow, but she may as well try it. Sam knew all the ins and outs of this area. Nell climbed out and stacked three rocks on top of each other, so he would know where she went.

This road was even worse. Nellie had no choice but to crawl along, trying to miss the worst ruts. Why didn't the drivers avoid it in the spring when it was still muddy? After what seemed like at least half an hour, forlorn-looking buildings appeared. No fancy automobile. Still, it would have been easy to hide it in the trees or behind a building. These were in better shape than Vienna had been.

"Let's scout around, Moonshine. Maybe he and my mother are here, or maybe not." Her poor mother. All her tales of Chicago would not have prepared her for being kidnapped. What a disaster! "Mother!" she called. "Mother! Are you here?"

Nell listened, trying to hear a human sound. A breeze ruffled aspen leaves that soughed in the air around the deserted mines. No birds chattered, so another car must have come this way. A doe peeked around an evergreen tree, her fawn close beside her. Maybe Nell was like the fawn, useless. Another call and the two animals sprang away.

"Where is the gold?" The voice startled Nell. She turned and there was Baker, not ten steps in front of her. She might have been back in Vienna.

"Where is my mother?"

"Give me the gold, and I'll give you your mother. I thought she was you, and you'd make a good hostage to get my gold back." He held a revolver in his hand, not aimed at Nell but at Moonshine, who was collared by Nell. "Don't let that dog near me."

"The sheriff has the gold. It doesn't belong to you, although I think you managed to get some of it. Or was that Hank?" A strange look crossed his face. Maybe he didn't know Hank had taken some of the gold?

"You were smart not to believe me back at Smiley Creek. Maybe I don't believe you now. Give me the key to your boot. You carried that water bag all over Kingdom Come. I bet it's still there."

"Go ahead and look. It's not locked. There is nothing of value in it now that Hank destroyed my camera." Nell watched as Baker sidled around to her auto. Moonshine stayed by her side, although she could feel him strain at his collar. He was more precious than gold and her camera. Moonshine turned his head and stared at one of the buildings. Was her mother there? Could Moonshine run fast enough to avoid being shot? Baker circled her auto and opened a back door. "Go Moonie. Get my mother!" She released his collar and he leaped toward the building he had watched. Baker straightened and before he could shoot, Moonshine had disappeared. Nell breathed a huge sigh of relief.

"She's all tied up. He won't help her." Baker strode to the passenger door and opened it. "Ha, there's a pack." He dumped it out on the seat. Her mother's things jingled and jangled and a few pieces dropped off the seat onto the ground. "Junk! You women are all alike." He turned to Nellie. "Where's your pack? You carried it everywhere, like it was tied to you."

"At home. I want to see if my mother is all right." She began to edge her way toward the building where Moonshine had gone.

"Sure. I'll tie you up, too. The sheriff can go back and get the gold, and I'll let you go. I know you called him. And maybe that one-eyed miner, too." He motioned with the gun. "Head on that way."

Nell knew this man was dangerous, and she didn't know how far to test him. He might not kill a woman as fast as he did his partners in crime. After all, he had only tied up her mother, not shot her in the head. Even the thought made her nauseous. She climbed two slanted steps to the building entrance. Her mother stood just inside and whispered. "Your dog untied me. What shall I do?"

"Mr. Baker." Nell raised her voice. "Please exchange me for my mother and let her go. You know my automobile doesn't contain anything of use to you." She followed that with a whisper. "Hide and take Moonie with you." Slipping through the opening, Nell said to her mother, "While he ties me up, go to the auto and drive away. The key is in the ignition."

"I can't drive!" Her mother hurried to a back door and pushed it open. It took a huge effort because the frame sagged. "Here, Moonshine."

Moonie looked at Nell and back at her mother. "Go, Moonshine."

Not ten seconds later, Baker came through the front entrance. The building they were in leaned slaunchwise. It might fall at any time. The man glanced quickly around. "Where did she go?"

"I don't know. Can't you keep track of your own hostages?" Nell stood in his view of the back door, she hoped. "There was no one here when I came in. Where is my mother?" She let her voice rise until she was almost shouting. "You monster. What have you done with my mother?"

The roof contained holes and sun shone through, making the space light inside. "There," Baker said. "There's the gag. And the rope. She managed to untie everything. I didn't hurt her one bit. What do you think I am?"

Nellie bit her lip so she wouldn't call him a murderer. "A thief," she said. She could taste blood in her mouth. "You stole gold from the Chinese workers." There. Her pack lay under a table where her mother must have been tied. She knew her revolver was in it. Back at Goldie's rooming house, she couldn't decide where to hide it. The pack seemed the safest place.

The sound of an automobile entering the mining area distracted Nell. Baker's head whipped around to look out the entrance of their building. It must be Sam, finally. An automobile door opened and then closed. Nell tip-toed to the table and sat on it. She kicked her pack further back in the shadows, so Baker wouldn't see it. Her mother must have grabbed it when the man pulled her out of Rosy's automobile instead of her own satchel.

"You stay here," Baker ordered Nell. "Or I'll shoot whoever drove up. Not a word." He stepped out of the entrance. "Who are you and what are you doing here?"

Sam's voice answered. "I could ask you the same thing, Baker. You know me. I'm the barkeep at the Stanley saloon. The one you owe a bunch of money to. I heard you had some gold, so I came to get what you owe me. Plus interest. There's probably an old assay scales around here somewhere."

"Ha, fat chance! That hogwash you sell isn't worth a cent!" He waved his gun back and forth. "Stay where you are if you don't want a hole in your head."

Nell leaned down and pulled her pack out. Inside, she found her revolver. She remembered Lulu's words: Don't aim it at anyone unless you intend to shoot it. "Baker," she said. "Keep on walking unless you want a hole in the back of your head."

He turned to face the revolver Nell aimed at him. "I intend to shoot if you so much as make any move except to walk out of here." Her hand shook, but she doubted he could see it in the cross bars the sun made through the roof. She stepped into a shadow. "Move. I'll be right behind you." As Nell neared the entrance, she called to Sam. "I have a gun, too. Baker is coming out toward you. I hope you have a good strong rope to hogtie him."

"That I do, Miss Burns. That I do." He backed up to his auto and pulled a rope from his boot, as he had turned to head back out of the area. "Did you find your mother?"

"She's in hiding, along with my dog. I'll go look once you have him tied. We can wait here for the sheriff."

"I want the gold," Sam said. "By rights, you owe it to me, Baker. Where is it?" He narrowed the gap to the man, his gun still aimed at him. "Turn around. Keep your gun on him, Miss Burns, while I tie him up." Sam laid his revolver on the ground and jerked Baker's arms back, circling them several times and then using the same rope to wrap around Baker's ankles, causing him to fall in the dust. He kicked at Sam, who toppled over and dropped his gun.

Nell walked up to Baker. "Do you want the same treatment you gave Bubba and Hank? A bullet in the forehead?" Both men looked up at her, open-mouthed. "Get up, Sam. I'm going to find my mother." She held her revolver aimed at Baker's head until Sam stood and jerked on the rope. Truly, Dean Baker was hog-tied. Sam grabbed the criminal's gun.

Arp. Arp. Moonshine trotted out from a mostly collapsed building. Margretta followed him.

"He has a bag in his mouth. I couldn't get it from him, Cora Nell. I'm sorry."

Nellie knelt to hold her dog. The bag was leather, but not unlike the lavender bags Moonshine had known earlier. "Here is at least some of the gold," she said, as she opened the drawstrings and felt inside. A few rock-like pieces shifted and she brought out one. It was a gold nugget. "Baker took the biggest pieces, no doubt." She patted Moonie. "Good dog."

Margretta held onto Nellie's shoulder. "Thank you for coming. I was afraid he was going to shoot me. I was so glad to see Moonshine!"

Standing, Nellie hugged her mother. "Here, you are about to collapse. Let me help you to the stairs over there, so you can recover. I'm so sorry this happened to you."

Sam the barkeep left Baker tied up in the dust, gathered up his own gun, and helped both Nellie and Margretta to the stairs to sit. "I'll find some water. You two ladies must be all done in." He grabbed the leather bag, sitting on the ground next to Nellie's revolver and Moonshine, who still guarded both. "I'll hold this bag until the sheriff arrives. He said he'd be on his way as soon as possible. I told him about your mother and you and that man over there." He offered the revolver to Nellie, who took it. "Thanks for your help, Miss Burns. You're a good man to have around in a pinch."

Chapter 22

LUNCHTIME CAME AND PASSED. NELLIE, Sam the barkeep, and Margretta spent the time seeking shade from the sun. They left Dean Baker tied in the dust. Sam found water in a bubbling creek behind one of the tumbled-down mine buildings. Nellie found a pan and some ceramic cups in another building and brought water to their captive. The rest she saved for themselves. Margretta stirred herself to fetch more water as the day grew warmer. Sam the barkeep walked around the area, poking here and there.

"This area used to have several mines. I don't know how successful they were. There were some camps over at the Josephus Lakes." He swept his arm around. "I knew some of the families who did some exploring for gold over that way. One fall, a rider came through and warned them a snowstorm was a-comin'. They piled all their belongings, four kids including a couple girls, into a wagon and got out. I'll be darned if there wasn't a couple feet of snow in that storm. Good thing they left, or they would've all died from exposure. The patriarch opened a hard goods store down in Meridian. Nice family, that. Never found much, though."

At last, a car came rumbling through on the road into the area where they waited. It was Charlie with the police automobile, and

Rosy was with him. "It looks as if you all took care of business up here. No need for a sheriff." He walked over to Baker, who struggled to sit up.

"Get me out of this! These people are plain nuts. I'm just a tourer and a fisherman." The man peered at the sheriff. "Hey, didn't we meet on the road into Vienna? You saw me. I was just fishing. Tried my luck there and left."

Rosy rounded the auto and shook his head. "Still lyin' like a rug." He stood next to Charlie. "That man killed Hank, maybe Bubba. Stole some of the gold. Kidnapped Margretta here." Both Nellie and Margretta had joined the two men. They shook dust out of their dresses. Rosy didn't note that they looked like they had been through the wringer.

"Not to mention what you did to me," Charlie said. Baker's face turned even redder than the sun had burned it.

"Moonshine found a leather pouch. It has gold nuggets in it. I suspect they are part of the Chinese cache of gold." Nellie pulled the bag out of her pack. She had persuaded Sam the barkeep to return it to her while they waited. Her revolver had gone back in when Charlie drove up. She turned to the sheriff. "Your hiding place wasn't so secret as we thought."

Charlie and Rosy replaced the hogtie with handcuffs and a rope around Baker's legs, then placed him behind the screen in the police auto. "Sam, thank you for your help. We will see about a reward for reporting the kidnapping and chasing out here." He shook the man's hand. "Nellie, climb in up front. Moonie can travel with you in the foot well. Rosy can drive Margretta back to Ketchum in his auto, the one you drove here. Your outing is finished for the day."

"Thank heavens," Nellie murmured. She assumed Charlie

wanted to scold her for coming to Stanley, but she didn't care. She just wanted to go home.

Rosy grinned like he'd just won a prize. "Mrs. Burns, I would be delighted to escort you back to Ketchum." Even Margretta looked happy about the arrangement. Nellie remembered the two of them had hit it off at the picnic at Last Chance Ranch.

* * *

Dean Baker moaned and whined for a while and then settled in. When Nellie looked back, his eyes were closed, and he was slumped sideways on the back seat. She hoped he had gone to sleep. Once he quieted down, Moonshine lay his head on Nellie's lap and slept.

"I'm glad you came, Charlie. I left Sam the barkeep with a load of instructions. I hurried off after Baker's auto." She wondered what would happen to it, but maybe he talked to Sam about arranging for its return to Hailey. They had talked a short while.

"Too bad your outing with your mother ended up this way. Stanley is such a beautiful area. Did you see any sheep on your way here?"

"No, I thought of finding Alphonso, but that meant the long drive toward Vienna. I don't care if I ever go there again."

"Have you talked to your mother about our getting married?" Charlie had gone to the heart of the matter.

"No. I invited her here so I could do that. I wanted her to meet you first. I've lived a carefree life, and I have been a little worried about marriage tying me down. I think you know that."

"Anybody who knows you, knows that." Charlie smiled. He reached over to pat her arm and then caressed it. "When do you plan to talk to her?"

"I don't know. She is so different from my memory of her as a mother. She's lovely, a flirt, carefree herself. I don't know if that is just a façade. I knew how hard she worked at the library, and I doubt that has changed. She always seemed so downtrodden." Nell remembered all the fights between her mother and father. She lived under his thumb until she threw him out. She nodded to herself. "I think she was stronger than I ever gave her credit for."

"You did not come out of a back alley, Nell. Like mother, like daughter." He glanced into the rear seat and turned back to the road ahead. They climbed toward Galena Pass. "Does she care that I am Basque, or Spanish? Some people dislike us." He kept his eyes forward.

"Heavens, no! I think she thinks you are exotic and she finds that intriguing." Nell, too, reached over and patted his leg. "Don't fall for my mother, though. She is too old for you." Nell laid her head against the back of her seat and within minutes fell asleep. She knew she was safe with Charlie.

In Ketchum, the sheriff dropped Nellie and Moonshine off so he could take Baker to the jail in Hailey. She waited a few moments and soon Rosy drove up with Margretta. The two of them entered the rooming house. Nellie no longer cared it might be seedy. It was her home. Margretta headed upstairs, and Moonshine tagged along with her. Nellie told Goldie a little about the morning's events and then she followed her mother into her own room. Margretta already had made herself at home.

"We should talk, my daughter. No wonder you love it here. This place is full of excitement, handsome men, guns, gold, and your lovely dog."

"I thought you were afraid of dogs."

"Not this one. Not after he helped get my gag loose and my ties." She petted him. He circled and dropped down beside where Margretta sat in the chair with her feet on the makeshift ottoman, a short stool with a pillow on it.

"I'm so sorry about what happened, Mother. What a way to be introduced to our lovely country." Nell crossed to the chair and hugged her mother. Nellie's guilt nearly overwhelmed her. She should not have gone into the saloon.

"Being married might be good for you. Calm you down. Keep you out of trouble."

"Don't count on it. I intend to keep working for Charlie, married or not. And running my portrait studio." She sat on the bed. "I've tried to explain that to him, but I'm not sure he really understands I am not going to be a housewife. Married, yes, but as equals."

Margretta gave a soft laugh. "We all think that, Cora Nell. It rarely happens. And he is Basque. Are their mothers independent, equal?" She closed her eyes for a moment. "Remember when I went to work at the library, thanks to Professor Blake? Your father had a complete fit. He left, and I found him at the saloon down the street, drunk as a fish. I told him if he wasn't going to support us, I had to." She waved her hand in front of her face, as if she were swatting flies. Her shoulders lifted and dropped. "I did what I should have done a long time ago. I told him to leave—don't come back. And he didn't."

Nell knew even better than her mother where her father had ended up. The city morgue. "Did you ever regret doing that?"

Margretta pinched her lips. "I regretted it because you lost your father. Otherwise, no."

"Do you think you'll ever get married again? You're pretty, have a good job, like a good time, I suspect." Nell had often waited for her mother to write that she would be marrying again.

"I don't think so. I like my freedom. So do you. Are you sure you want to get married?" She leaned forward. "You always said you never would."

This time, Nell laughed shortly. "I know I did. Charlie changed my mind." Being close to him, having his arms around her, feeling safe and loved, and more, had changed her mind. She loved his dry sense of humor, his steadfast attention to the law, his sense of right and wrong.

"Tell me, what changed your mind?" Her mother appeared eager to know.

Nell repeated the litany that had just flowed through her mind.

"I hope you are physically attracted, too. That can get you through tough times, but the sense of humor might be the most important of all." Margretta beckoned to Nell, who sat next to Moonshine on the floor, her arms wrapped around her legs. "I don't have much wisdom to impart to you, Nellie. But your sheriff seems like the right man for you. He trusts and loves you, I believe. It is clear to me you feel the same way. Do you know anything about his background?"

"But didn't you trust and love my father? What went wrong?" She wasn't certain how much to tell her mother about Charlie's background—his family in Spain, his stint of sheepherding, his love affair with Gwynn Campbell's daughter years ago. His son, Matthew.

"I can blame alcohol," Margretta said. Her face wrinkled into a frown. "But we were too young and, in the end, didn't really trust each other." Her eyes seemed to see into the past. "And, in the end, this is your decision to make, yours and Charlie's." Margretta pushed herself out of the chair. "I'm going to take a nap. Maybe our next adventure could be a little less exciting." She leaned to kiss her daughter's head.

The next morning Nell arrived at the dining room after most of the boarders had left. She expressed surprise to find Charlie and Margretta deep in conversation at the table. Goldie was nowhere in sight, so Nell entered the kitchen to see if any breakfast remained. No Goldie there either. Hmmm, she thought. Someone had schemed with someone else. She found a plate of scrambled eggs and toast in the mostly cool oven and decided that was for her. She carried it into the dining room and sat at the other end of the table from the two someones.

"Hello, dear," her mother said. "How are you this morning, Cora Nell?"

"Hello, dear," Charlie said. Her mother and the sheriff looked at each other and smiled.

"I am only called Cora Nell around here when someone is upset with me—Charlie, Rosy, Goldie. My friend, Sammy, always calls me Miss Burns." She felt her face flush. "Even Gwynn Campbell says Cora Nell when he wants my attention for some perceived wrong." Warm tea sat on the sideboard, so she helped herself and sat again. "What are you two plotting? Our daily adventure? I thought the Guyer Hot Springs might be a good respite for us."

"You declined to tell me much about Charlie, so I asked him here to answer all my questions. He surely did, and then some." Margretta's eyes grew rounder. "It's a good thing you two are getting married. Maybe you won't have so many close calls if he keeps track of you."

"I prefer to think I am learning my lessons and getting wiser," Nell answered. "Therefore, I won't have so many close calls. Having a revolver helps, too. Besides, Moonshine considers it his job to keep track of me. He is good at it."

Charlie laughed out loud. "I am off to work, Mrs. and Miss Burns. Have a good time at the hot springs. I wish I could join you, but I must transfer a prisoner to Twin Falls to the jail there. It is much more secure."

"And the gold? Does Sammy get any for finding it?"

"He has stopped by once or twice." Charlie stood and neared Nellie. He looked around and kissed her cheek. Nellie could feel herself blush. A kiss in front of her mother embarrassed her.

"Why don't you two set a date?" Margretta asked.

Chapter 23

AS HAILEY DID NOT HAVE a Joss House, Sammy held his mother's funeral outdoors where the other Chinese people lived near the Big Wood River in makeshift housing and tents. One Chinese man who practiced Confucianism and one Chinese man who practiced Buddhism conducted the ceremony together. The remaining Chinese in the camp brought food and some of their last precious belongings. Sammy was touched for his mother. These Chinese had known her better than he did. It was a mishmash of a farewell for Mother, but he did not think she would have minded. As long as his father's skull could be with her, her ghost would not complain.

Earlier in the week, Sammy climbed to a high ridge north of Hailey and dug a grave for her. Sagebrush grew on the slopes on both sides of the grave, hugging it with silver-green leaves. Yellow flowers bloomed in bunches with many leaves shaped like arrows. She would like the beauty and the threat. Sam borrowed a shovel from Joe High Sing but told him not to come. Sammy suspected him, still, of killing Hung Lui. What would Hung's ghost say if Sam associated with the killer. Sam was still waiting for his bones to cleanse so he could send them to Guangdong.

Sammy had ordered a marble tombstone for his mother and also a marble slab so her bones would never escape. She wanted to be buried in the valley, and he thought the view from the high ridge would satisfy her ghost. Bunches of grass spread under the sage, and the scent of the sage smelled bitter and sweet at the same time. Such a spot suited his honored mother.

Miss Burns came to the funeral ceremony, the only white person among the Chinese. She wore white, the Chinese color for mourning. After the ceremony, Sammy wrapped his mother in a silken robe from her house, tucking his father's skull on her chest. He carried her to Miss Burns's automobile, and they drove to the canyon north of Hailey. Sammy climbed up the ridge with his mother's corpse. It was light as air, she was so tiny and shrunken. Miss Burns climbed, too. Sam had warned her what he planned to do. She said she wanted to come.

The hike caused their breathing to speed up but was not difficult. Sammy laid his mother in her grave. Then he returned to the automobile to get the tombstone. He did not know when his honored non-mother was born, but only the date she died. He subtracted how old he thought she was—sixty years. Those dates appear on the tombstone, along with her name, Opal Ah Kee, and the words "Honored wife of Ah Kee and honored mother of Sam Ah Kee." Sammy remembered enough Chinese characters to inscribe a few that said something like "May she rest in peace." That was a phrase many white people said about their dead ancestors.

Miss Burns placed a flower on Sammy's wrapped mother. She dropped a handful of dirt, and then Sam buried her. The hole for the tombstone took longer than the grave itself. The slab for the top of the grave was not ready, so he would install it later.

"I cannot but think about the night we sought your father's bones," Miss Burns said. "The moon shone so alabaster." She rubbed her hand on the top of the tombstone. "This marble is just as white. I am glad your mother did not want her bones sent to China. I will always think of all these bones—your father's, Hung Lui's, your mother's—as moon bones." She folded her hands in front of her chest and bent her head. After several minutes, she lifted her face. "Would you like to stay longer? I can come back for you."

"No, Miss Burns. I have done what my honored mother and my religion have instructed me to do. I will come another day to spend time with her. By the end of the Hungry Ghost Festival, I will leave and not return."

"The Hungry Ghost Festival? When is that, and what is it?"

"That is the time when ghosts return to their owners. It is in the seventh month of the Lunar Year." Sam explained that food and presents are offered to the ghosts of the departed during that month in the fall. So few Chinese were left in Hailey, he wasn't certain the festival would be held, but he would observe it and then leave. Sammy did not tell her about the string of lustrous pearls belonging to his mother that he would bury under the marble slab when it was ready.

"I will miss you, Sammy. I am sorry you are leaving. Will you send me your address once you are settled somewhere else?" Miss Burns touched his arm.

Sammy nodded, although he would never do that. Getting too close to white people always brought bad luck to Chinese. Still, Miss Burns had been kind to him, and she mourned his mother. He would at least let her know when he was settled. Maybe someday he would be happy again, the way he was with both a father and a mother and a friend. Now all three were gone. Like his mother, Sammy did not want to return to Guangdong in China.

When Sammy and Miss Burns returned to the Ah Kee house, Miss Burns opened the boot. "I have something for you from the sheriff," she said. She pulled out a machete. "I don't think this is yours, but the sheriff believes it was used to kill Hung Lui. He thought you might be able to decipher the Chinese character on the hilt. If so, you should give him the information as it might lead to Hung Lui's killer." She handed it over. In addition, she offered a small pouch. "This is from the Chinese men we rescued at Vienna. They passed on their thanks for finding their gold. They will not be returning to Vienna or anywhere in this valley either. The eldest said if you go to Boise, you should visit the Joss House there and register your name. They will help you with anything you need."

Sammy took possession of both the machete and the bag. Maybe the sheriff was a good white man like Miss Burns was a good white woman. Sam knew they intended to marry. If he hadn't left by the time they did marry, he would give them a Chinese blessing. "The sheriff is a good man." With the gold, Sam could now pay a rental fee until he moved away. Boise might be a good place to stay. The Chinese seemed mostly accepted there. He wondered what made the difference between being burned out of a home by white men and being settled in a place where white people let Chinese stay. Maybe he would find out.

The machete's blade had turned black. Sammy soaked it in water and soap and scrubbed it. The water turned pink, from blood, he assumed. Because Hung Lui had been killed with something like this machete and not a bullet from a gun, he had assumed it was a Chinaman who killed him. Why the Chinese said a white man did it when the sheriff asked about the slashing of the throat, he did not know. Maybe they knew the man who did it. Maybe it was a matter of a tong dispute, and no Chinese wants to get into the middle of such an affair.

A Chinese symbol had been scratched into the hilt of the blade. Once the blood soaked away, Sammy could read it. Even though he was no longer familiar with many Chinese characters, he knew this one. The sheriff wanted the name. Sam wanted revenge for Hung Lui.

Back along the river path Sammy hurried to get to the Chinese camp. He even knew which tent where the man stayed. Sam entered it to find no one. Instead, he found a burnished wood container, like ones that held his father's powders. Sam opened it. It, too, was empty. He knew then that his mother's coins once filled it. She had paid this man to murder Hung Lui, so the secret of his mother and father would not be told. The secret that Sam Ah Kee was stolen away from his true mother would never be revealed in *Melica*, as Hung Lui called it. Why had he not told Sammy? Had he gone to Mother and threatened to tell? Why would he do that? Sammy would never know now.

The tent ruffled and Joe High Sing entered. He saw the machete in Sam's hand.

"I did not do it!" Joe dropped to his knees. "I did not do it."

Sammy lifted the machete to strike Joe dead.

"I paid a white man to do it. I could not do it." He pointed to the wood container. "Your mother paid me to do it and I could not. The white man slashed my leg with my own machete. I gave him some of the money, and he did it." He hung his head, waiting for Sam to slash his neck and behead him.

Sammy could not do it. He did not know if Joe lied.

"Then you must come with me and tell the sheriff what you have done and what the white man did. If you do not, I will give him the machete anyway, and he will come after you." Sammy placed the point of the machete in the ground. Joe did not know Sam could not slash him. "You owe this to me and to my honored mother."

"The sheriff is a white man. I am Chinese. He will never believe me. He will throw me in jail because he will think I killed Hung Lui." Joe stayed on his knees.

"If you tell the truth, he will believe you. He has been hunting Hung's killer all along." Sammy hoped he was not wrong. "Why did my mother pay you to do this terrible deed?"

"Your mother said Hung Lui had played you as a fool. Also, that he knew secrets and would tell you. She did not tell me what the secrets were, or she would have had me killed, too. Your mother was a vengeful person." He studied Sammy's face. "But you knew that already." He looked at his hands, which were dirty. "Your mother helped many people after your father died. She helped my sister."

He did not have to say anything more. Sammy had thought he didn't know his mother, but everything Joe said about her was true. Sammy already missed his honored mother.

Chapter 24

GWYNN PICKED NELLIE UP AT the rooming house in Ketchum. He drove a large automobile, a new, shiny model. That reminded Nell, she should ask the rancher about any old autos hanging around his property in Twin Falls. She needed one for herself, now that she and Charlie had found a place to live in Hailey. He and she had already argued about her maintaining her studio at Goldie's, at least for the time being. Charlie said it was a waste of gasoline and what would she drive, anyway?

Nell brought a suitcase filled with her dress, shoes, hat and veil. Sammy was bringing flowers from one of the Chinese gardens in Hailey. He wanted that to be a present. He said he owed her so much and could never repay her. Nell had taken his hands and said, "Your being here is present enough, Sammy. I owe you, too." He had removed his Oriental hat and bowed to her. Tears threatened for such a humble gesture to her.

Margretta and Nell had finally visited all the places she planned. When her mother left, Nell had accompanied Charlie to Twin Falls to tell the authorities there all she knew of the events in July. She had introduced Charlie and Jacob and talked to Jacob about a new camera, used so it wouldn't be so expensive. She and Charlie took the train once and drove another time. Charlie had to go a third time. The trial for Dean Baker would be in October.

Charlie had said he would get himself to Last Chance Ranch. Rosy, his sister, and the boys would already be there, although school had begun in Ketchum and the boys had moved down. Rosy didn't want to leave just yet. A few other people had been invited, people Charlie had picked up in his job or Nellie had photographed in her studio. When she wrote out invitations, the number of people they both knew surprised her. Franklin and Mabel motored all the way from Twin Falls, too, bringing Maria and picking up Goldie. She and Henry had delivered a "passel of food" and drink the day before, much of which was stashed in the river to keep it cold.

The sun warmed the day, although chilly nights had already turned most of the leaves on aspens and cottonwoods and maples. The colors warmed Nell: yellow, pumpkin, scarlet, burgundy shrubs, and golden grass. Only sagebrush stayed the same. Deep yellow rabbit brush flourished everywhere and some of them now looked like sheep in the fields with their rabbit-tail-bushy seed pods. Scattered leaves left their scent in the air. A perfect day.

The only things that marred the day were thoughts of those who weren't with them: Hung Lui, Opal, even Joe, who was being held as an accessory to Hung's murder, although Sammy said he would be released. She hoped Baker would spend years and years in jail. The three Chinese from the mill said they would come, but so far, Nell had not seen them. She had written Pearl and Ned, her friends from the Stanley Basin, in Oregon, but received no response. Maybe they were no longer together. Lulu closed the Galena Store so she could come. Jacob Levine planned to attend with his ex- and now current fiancée who had returned from the East. He promised to take photographs.

"Nell, are you nervous?" Gwynn had opened the auto windows

so the breeze swirled in.

"No, but I will be if my hair gets mussed." She held onto her head and was glad she still had her flapper hairdo.

"Oops, sorry." He rolled up his window and glanced at her with a wink. "You are the prettiest thing in this whole Big Wood River Valley."

Nellie could feel her cheeks burning. "I hope Charlie thinks so."

"Oh, he will, or else he's blind." Gwynn had finally made his peace with Charlie over Gwynn's daughter Lily.

It was her presence at Last Chance Ranch that held Rosy there, Nell surmised. Even she could feel Lily when she walked inside the house, but especially when she inhaled the lavender scent both outside and in. Rosy had given her the Chinese robe that had belonged to Lily. It had been a gift to Lily from Ah Kee, the herbalist. Nellie imagined herself wearing that robe for the event today. The Chinese who attended might have been shocked.

When Nellie and Gwynn stepped out of his automobile, the scent of lavender over-powered them. Gwynn released Moonshine from the rear seat. The purple haze on the whole front field had faded somewhat and bees no longer swarmed among the blossoms. Fall offered colors on the one hand and swiped them away with the other. They walked through the field to the front porch. Rosy and the boys waited. Moonie rushed to the boys, who petted and hugged him.

"Nellie, we picked as many flowers as we could find and some branches with pretty leaves and put them all over the house. If it is too hot outside, it will be all right inside." Matt swung his arms and Campbell jumped up and down. "We can hardly wait!" Then they brought out a leafy garland and placed it around Moonshine's neck. "Moonie is our hero. He deserves to have colors, too!"

Rosy's sister Esther came out on the porch. She carried a huge vase of roses and baby's breath. "That Chinese man brought all these roses. Where shall I put them?" She wrinkled her nose, but her mouth split in a big grin. "They smell so sweet, but I'm afraid I will sneeze the whole time if they are too near me." And she sneezed, nearly dropping the vase.

"Matt, take the bunch of posies and put them on a bale of hay down by the river," Rosy said. He pointed to several bales situated near aspen trees by the Big Wood River. "You may have to stay inside, Esther. The rabbitbrush is going off like mad." He turned to Nellie. "A bunch of people are sittin' and standin' inside because of the sun out here," he said, using a low voice, but everyone could hear. "Charlie ain't here, yet. Does he know today is the day?"

Nell hoped so. Leaving her on her wedding day would be humiliating and heart breaking.

She knew he would not do that to her. "I'll go upstairs and change my clothes. I am sure he will arrive soon." As she walked through the house, the long room with the fireplace at the end, she waved to friends and a few strangers who were friends of Charlie's. She pushed through the door leading to the stairs and climbed them. The boys' bunkroom had been cleaned to a fare thee well, she thought. Esther must have made the boys do that. The dress her mother had helped her find in the Sears Roebuck catalog flowed with lawn and lace, reaching to her ankles and tucked in around her waist perfectly, as did the shoes. The puffed sleeves narrowed to hug her wrists, and the high collar of lace graced her face. Around her shoulders she placed a delicate silk shawl Gwynn had given to her. At her bosom, she pinned a brooch from Sammy that had belonged to his mother. She decided not to wear the veil. It seemed too much. She was ready.

Back downstairs, Charlie still had not arrived. Jacob wasn't there either. She had looked forward to his taking photographs, but maybe his fiancée decided she didn't want to come. Nell looked at Gwynn. "Maybe we should go to the river?" A helpless feeling arose inside and was beginning to overwhelm her. She remembered Gwynn's leg pained him. "No, you stay here. I'll walk by myself."

Rosy, bless his heart, had scythed a path to the river through gold grasses and the dried remains of wildflowers. Nell loved the fall in this high desert country. The smell of sun on dust, the dried autumn leaves, and the soothing sound of the river as it flowed south, wrapped around her. Where was Charlie? She had many memories of Last Chance Ranch, not all of them good, but it had seemed the right place to get married, to be surrounded by her friends and the boys. She remembered, too, how lonely she had felt her first few months in the small towns of the Wood River Valley. She wasn't lonely anymore, unless, of course, Charlie failed to show. But he would come. There would be a reason he was late.

"Nellie!" Rosy's deep voice traveled the distance to where she lingered by the river, admiring the aspen trees on the other side.

Nellie glanced toward the house. Rosy came down the path to her side. "Charlie's here. Time to come up, Missy. Are you ready?"

Nellie glanced down at her dress. "Yes. I am nervous. I've never done this before."

Rosy laughed. "Good thing. You'll be fine." He wrapped an arm around her shoulders. "At least, this ways, you'll be staying here. Maybe not at Last Chance Ranch," he said, "but in the Wood River Valley."

"Rosy," Nellie hugged his arm and then held it as they walked up the slope. "I've wondered. Who is under the 'Unknown' grave sign in the woods? The boys showed it to me."

Rosy had a tanned lined face, but even so, he blushed. "Do you remember that package I delivered to the Triumph mine the day we headed up there?" He stopped and looked at Nell.

Nell tried to remember. "Oh, yes. You gave it to Gladys, and she stuck it in a file drawer."

"I got it back and buried it here. The least I could do for my old friend Jack."

Nell frowned a moment. "Ah." She nodded her head. "I thought that was what you carried. I'm glad you buried it." She hugged his arm again and they continued their walk.

Charlie met her at the house and pulled her to him. "Sorry, I am late. There was something that needed doing, and I had to do it. I'll tell you later." He wore the Basque vest he had worn in North Idaho. His clean-shaven face looked so tan in the sunlight, she could hardly resist placing her hand on his cheek. On his head perched a brand new Stetson.

Rosy announced: "It's not too hot. Let's all walk to the river. I fixed up a trail." He poked his head inside the door to the living area. "Up, up, up. We're all a-goin' to the river. Guests first." He stepped outside. "Gwynn, you wait with me and Nellie and Goldie here. Charlie, you might as well go stand in front of the guests so they can all get a good look at you before you become a married man." He grinned. "Single men are becomin' purty rare around here, with the exception of Gwynn and me."

Goldie served as Nellie's matron of honor. She walked down next. Nellie's mother had not been able to return for the wedding, but she and Nell had made their promises to each other. They would not let so much time pass before they visited each other again.

Once everyone waited by the river, Gwynn and Rosy placed Nellie between them and walked with her to meet Charlie. Nellie thought her heart would burst with joy. Even Alphonso had managed to arrive just after Charlie. Jacob stood with the guests, too. His fiancée seemed to smile with relief. Jacob moved to his camera, set on a tripod, so he could photograph the marrying couple as they stood in front of all the guests.

Gwynn, as the oldest of all those present, stepped to the front to face Charlie and Nellie. He read the marriage service from an Episcopal prayer book. Charlie and Nell said their vows to each other. Charlie slipped the engagement ring back on Nellie's hand as her wedding ring. Sammy had found his father's gold ring and given it to Nell to give to Charlie. And then they were married.

"Whoop-de-do!" Rosy called. "Let's all go back to the house for a big surprise!"

Nell had no idea what he was talking about. She thought her marriage was a big surprise for most everyone. It certainly was to her.

On the front porch stood a large box, covered with silver paper and silver bows. Charlie nudged Nellie forward. "Your first job as my wife—unwrap this giant present." Even he had a wide grin on his face. Everyone else did, too.

Nellie pulled on the ribbon to untie it. She slipped her hand under the wrapping paper and slid it off. She lifted the cardboard flaps and looked inside. "Oh my!" Tears slipped down her cheeks. "Oh my. Charlie, you did this?"

Charlie joined her. "Rosy, Jacob, Goldie, and I did this. Take it out!"

Nell leaned into the box and stood up, holding a brand new Premo camera in her hands. It wasn't as small as her broken camera had been. It filled her arms. She placed it on the table on the porch and leaned into the box again. She lifted a new tripod, boxes of film, and other accoutrements. "Oh my! Thank you, thank you!"

An automobile traveled through the gate and up to the house. Gwynn stepped out, holding a key. "And here is my wedding present to the two of you, although I expect Nellie will get the most use out of it."

Nellie recognized it as the auto Gwynn had been driving until he purchased the new one he used to pick her up at Goldie's that morning. She glanced around all her friends and saw Alphonso, his white teeth gleaming in his face. He must have driven it from Ketchum. Everyone, it seemed, had been making plans behind her back to surprise her and make her wedding day extra-special.

Nell swept her arms toward her friends and stepped back into Charlie's arms. "How can I ever thank all of you enough?" She hugged Charlie, and he held her close.

"My additional vow to you is to keep you safe," he said. "Your mother made me say that. And I will not interfere with your independence. You made me say that."

The guests laughed. Charlie leaned to kiss Nellie on her lips, and she kissed him back. Moonshine barked and licked Nellie's hand. A round of clapping passed through their friends, echoed by the clattering of gold quaking aspen leaves.

Author's Note

IN THE LATE 1800s in Idaho, approximately thirty percent of its population was Chinese, mostly men from the Guangdong area of China. The total population of the state was only around 15,000. Many Chinese traveled to Washington, Oregon, and Idaho, after completing work on the railroad. Others came because of the gold rushes in Idaho, seeking their fortunes in Gold Mountain, as America was called. Most planned to make their fortune and return to China. A Chinatown in Boise grew rapidly, although in later years and by the turn of the 20th Century, the Chinese population had diminished to much smaller numbers, partly because gold claims dissipated and the Chinese were not allowed to work them anyway. Hence, most Chinese set up laundries and restaurants. As with most of the Northwest, harassment of the "Orientals" or "Celestials" as they were often known as, drove them back to China or to larger cities on the West Coast. The white population of Central Idaho also participated in efforts to oust Chinese in Twin Falls and Hailey, which were not always successful.

In addition to several massacres of Chinese gold miners in Idaho mentioned in this story, there were incidents of crime among the Chinese themselves, often in the context of tongs, benevolent associations of Chinese men. The Chinese Exclusion

Act of 1882 was passed by Congress at the behest of western states. Enforcement was lackadaisical for a number of years, and Chinese who were returning to America were allowed back in. The Scott Act, passed in 1888 excluded all Chinese, so the number immigrating to America diminished.

My sources for much of the Chinese information and lore came from several books: *Chinatown: Boise, Idaho, 1870 – 1970* by Arthur A. Hart; *Ghosts of Gold Mountain: The Epic Story of the Chinese Who Built the Transcontinental Railroad* by Gordon H. Chang; and *Massacred for Gold: The Chinese in Hells Canyon* by R. Gregory Nokes. The book *Stanley-Sawtooth Country* by Esther Yarber with the assistance of Edna McGown provided source material for the Stanley Basin area. Our visits to the ghost towns of Custer and Bonanza in the Stanley Basin spurred some of the ideas for *Moon Bones* and provided background information. As with my other mysteries set in Idaho in the 1920s, the Center for Regional History at The Community Library in Ketchum, Idaho, provided assistance with other resources, including legal documents and books.

The burial near the end of the story is rumored to exist in an area north of Hailey, Idaho, known as Indian Creek. Although I have not seen it, I have read first-hand accounts of hikes to the site. The fact of its existence along with our visits to ghost towns encouraged my imagination for parts of the story in this book. We did visit Vienna itself, but all the buildings have disappeared. The entrance to the mine above the town is still there.

Acknowledgments

GHOST TOWNS DOT THE LANDSCAPE of central Idaho. A few, like Silver City south of Boise, host visitors and locals alike with a hotel and sights to see. No mining takes place in any of the towns in the area. Others, like Custer and Bonanza, north of Ketchum, represent the more usual old mining towns with a few restored houses and plaques giving their history. Falling down or rusted mine buildings and mills appear in a few of the once active towns. Historical societies make efforts to educate visitors about the thriving communities in their heydays. Towns in or near Hailey and Ketchum and in the Stanley Basin have disappeared completely. Vienna is one of those. Only a sign and a mine entrance still exist. Forests, grasses, and occasional flowers have filled what were once streets, saloons, assay offices, tents, and other structures once occupied by up to 200 people, mostly men.

My husband and I have visited many of the old towns, exploring for what was left, and taking photographs of remains. We stayed in Silver City and wandered the paths of Custer and Bonanza. The only visible remnants related to the Chinese population were sites noted as laundries or a restaurant. I thank Mary Tyson and Kelley Moulton who found archival materials in The Community Library and its Center for Regional History in Ketchum, Idaho, including documents, all handwritten, of conflicts with Chinese in the area, photographs of old buildings of Vienna, and photographs of Chinese who worked near the mines.

Once again, I thank my writing colleagues, Belinda Anderson and Mary Murfin Bayley, who read the manuscript and gave me solid suggestions for improvement and cheered along my efforts. I cannot imagine writing and solving mysteries without their assistance. Thanks to Wendy Jaquet and also to John Lundin, a writer and researcher of local history, for his assistance in furnishing information about the Chinese caves in Bellevue, Idaho, and related stories. My husband, Gerry Morrison, is always my first reader and his red pen guides my stories, particularly as they relate to the camera used by Nellie Burns and her photographic efforts.

My Author's Note at the end lists the sources I used for Chinese life and rituals in Idaho, as well as information about the Vienna mine and the Stanley Basin. We live close to many of the sites mentioned in the book and in this acknowledgment. It is always fun and interesting to imagine life in this area in the 1920s.

Encircle Publications is now publishing my earlier books in paperback and ebooks. All four will be available in those formats as well as this fifth novel, *Moon Bones*. Covid has slowed down the new formats and the progress of this new one. I hope we are back to fairly normal times, but as we all know, Covid has its own timetable. Deirdre Wait has been particularly instrumental in my transition to Encircle and I appreciate her support. Like Nellie in her life, I am moving into a new phase, too.

As always, I thank my husband for his continued support and editing and photographic skills. We enjoy our life in Idaho and especially exploring places where Nellie Burns and her retinue can continue to solve mysteries.

About the Author

JULIE WESTON grew up in Idaho and practiced law for many years in Seattle, Washington. Her short stories and essays have been published in *IDAHO Magazine*, *The Threepenny Review*, *River Styx*, and *Rocky Mountain Game & Fish*, among other journals and magazines, and in the anthology *Our Working Lives*. Her book, *The Good Times Are All Gone Now: Life, Death and Rebirth in an Idaho Mining Town* (University of Oklahoma Press, 2009) won Honorable Mention in the 2009 Idaho Book of the Year Award. She appeared on a C-Span2/Book TV interview in December, 2013. Both an essay and a short story were nominated for Pushcart Prizes. She is the author of the Nellie Burns and Moonshine Mysteries: *Moonshadows*, a Finalist in the Mary Sarton Literary Awards; *Basque Moon*, winner of the 2017 WILLA Award in Historical Fiction; *Moonscape*, Bronze winner of the INDIE Foreword Awards; *Miners' Moon*, a Finalist in the Will Rogers Medallion Awards for Mystery; and *Moon Bones*, published by Encircle Publications in October, 2022.

She and her husband, Gerry Morrison, now live in south-central Idaho where they ski, write, photograph, and enjoy the outdoors. You can learn more by visiting www.julieweston.com.

If you enjoyed reading this book,
please consider writing your honest review
and sharing it with other readers.

Many of our Authors are happy to participate in
Book Club and Reader Group discussions.
For more information, contact us at info@encirclepub.com.

Thank you,
Encircle Publications

For news about more exciting new fiction, join us at:

Facebook: www.facebook.com/encirclepub

Instagram: www.instagram.com/encirclepublications

Twitter: twitter.com/encirclepub

Sign up for Encircle Publications newsletter and specials:
eepurl.com/cs8taP

CPSIA information can be obtained
at www.ICGtesting.com
Printed in the USA
JSHW042217220922
30792JS00001B/3